JOYFIELD

RUDSDALE FERRIER

DEDICATION

I dedicate this book to the woman I wish I'd known from the first moment I opened my eyes upon this earth, and the one I pray is beside me when I take my last breath, the only woman I will ever truly love, my beautiful wife, Tracy.

CHAPTER

RUDSDALE FERRIER

Books by R.M. FERRIER

The Crow Flies South For The Winter

The House Of The Black Goat

Cemetery Side Road

The Crow's Nest Lies Beneath The Snow

Murder Down The French Line

Kentucky Rose Garden

Road Kill

CHAPTER 1

THE VOICE OF JOY

All that is left is the silence... The sky is blue, the sun is shining, yet there is emptiness in everything I see. I can't hear the voice of Joy anymore... I see the fields of green all around me. The trees have blossomed and the flowers are rampant in bloom, but all I notice is her absence. We've been together since we were infants, but now we part ways for good.

Joy Abigail Summerstein, my dearest friend and loyal companion throughout all my boyhood adventures over the course of my young life, has been laid to rest today. She died at the unfortunate age of thirteen. I say unfortunate because it was the last year she got. She will never have any more, nor will I be given more time with her. The two of us couldn't have been closer. We played between the haystacks in Barrett's Meadow going on eight summers. Though I know it's too early for formal contemplation, I believe we would have married one day. I couldn't imagine a life without her, and now here I have that exact unholy gift wrapped up and delivered to me to open and stare at for the remainder of my life.

I walk between my father and mother, back down to the road.

"Your little friend has been left behind in the

cemetery to sleep," my father provokes from the low, gravelly grumble in his throat. "You will have to find a new companion to play with now, or better yet, forget about playing altogether and start to seriously consider your work."

My mother looks upon me and smiles.

"It's much too early for that. It will take time to get over. There is no denying that you two children were very close. You can't just forget."

I shake my head with solemn conviction.

"I will never forget her. I loved her…"

"You will get over her," my father reinforces upon my beliefs. "There is no point wasting your time over things you can't change. Worry about the days out in front of you, not what has been lost to the past. You've lost your little friend. Now all you can do is forget her and move on."

My gentle mother reaches out to me with a warm embrace.

"I know it's not easy, my boy, but all things heal with time."

No words hold the power to make me feel better, no matter how well intended, for I know I've lost my Joy.

I spend the days that follow searching the countryside for some sign of life, be it in the hills, the orchards or the lilac springs. I've tried to replace my Joy with sunshine... and long days spent wandering in the lowland woods that reach down on all sides of our little farm up on Cabot's Hill. Such pursuits aren't much good for forgetting; I used to do all those things with my friend. All the places we used to play together are full of ghosts now – hers, mine and at least a half dozen of our unborn children's. Everything we'll never get a chance to do together is all I can think of. And how much of a shame is it to be stuck in so deep a rut as that? But I can't help it; I thoroughly loved that little girl. I swore I would marry her one day. I suppose we ought to be careful about the promises we make to ourselves; some of them are impossible to keep.

Today I find myself out on Cutler Road. I'm on my way back from an auction. My father was there to bid on a thrasher, and I was sent to deliver him a message. A man was to drop by our farm to look at a horse and my mother wanted my father home by four o'clock. She wasn't going to have strangers hanging around the place without him there. Strange men are not to be trusted.

I got to the auction too late. It was already over and the last stragglers were collecting their treasures and loading them into their trucks and wagons. My father had left before my arrival. I would have seen him on the road if I had taken it. Since I'd come cross country through the fields and meadows, I had missed him entirely.

Having failed in my quest, I did not linger at

the sale. I was in no mood for being social. One kindly neighbour stopped to say hello, but I pretended I didn't hear him and kept on walking. He went back to loading furniture into his truck and pretended that he hadn't bothered in the first place.

It is not my intention to offend anyone, though I do not wish to be inundated with their sympathetic charms. Everyone around here knows that Joy Summerstein and I were very best friends. We went everywhere together. We were never apart. I suppose it seems odd seeing one without the other. I shouldn't blame people for noticing something amiss... and I don't so much, really. I just can't stand being talked to about it right now, that's all I'm getting at.

I've been dragging my heels and kicking at the gravel for a good half mile since leaving the Scott farm where the auction was held. I'm in no hurry home, and my progress in that direction has shown as much. I'm too far lost in my head, thinking about the things Joy and I used to do together, and I'm not paying close attention to my surroundings. What's the difference? I've seen all these fields before. One hay field is pretty much the same as the next... Each field of grain grows towards the sky just like the one beside it, and if I look too closely, it only makes me remember what I've lost.

Something makes me look up now for a reason I can't put my finger on specifically. Perhaps I simply desire to know how near I am to being home for supper. Maybe it's no more than being tired of staring at the ground. However I choose to justify it in my head, it doesn't matter; something unusual to my senses corrals my attention just as soon as my eyes skate across the fields to the horizon. Looking out over the waving barley flood, I become aware of something I have not seen before. A barn waits for my gaze to reach it in the distance, though I have never seen a barn quite like it. I am dumbfounded by how I have not noticed it until now. Its sheer mass is unmistakable. It towers above the earth like a fortress asserting its dominion over the land. I swear I've never seen such a barn in all my life. Its rafters reach towards the sky a good hundred feet into the air, and its bulk covers up at least two acres of ground. It's not a new building. Its boards are all grey and well worn by the weather. In fact, it looks quite old. Some of its boards have gone missing, and in places, its beams have begun to spread.

I'm amazed by its presence… I'm amazed at how I could have missed it before. I've travelled up and down this road five days a week for the last eight years – my schoolhouse lies but a mile further down the road, yet I have never seen it. How can that be possible, I beg to know? Have I never bothered to look up in that direction? Often a dense fog lies over those fields. That might have hidden it, I suppose. It's clear today. Perhaps the light is just right for noticing things usually missed.

I feel an overwhelming urge to explore today. I know it's getting late and I should be home for supper, but there is still enough daylight lingering in afternoon to see what that place is all about.

I leave Cutler Road behind me and cut a pathway through the hay stand. Four fields in and I finally reach it. Upon seeing it up close enough to lay my hand on the rough boards layered across its flank, I'm relieved to see it wasn't an apparition. It's made out of real wood and real stone. I wasn't just seeing things brought on by sunstroke from too much time spent out in the hot afternoon.

As I gaze up at the towering mass above me, a rush of excitement pervades my senses. I can't wait to climb up into the hayloft to see what's inside. I only wish… I have to be careful now… but I only wish that Joy were here. There would be nothing grander than being able to explore this place together. It seems like it was all we did over the course of our young lives – not that I am very old now. I am but thirteen. The primary difference is that now I'm all alone… so all alone that I find a barn door open just enough to squeeze inside… and all alone I begin to climb a ladder leading up into the haymow. It's a long ways up. The loft is full of hay – and full of haymows to house it. The space inside the barn is expansive. Just as soon as I reach one mow, there is another lying just beyond. Each is packed full of baled hay and laying a foundation for the next. I find myself racing from one mow to another… climbing over stacks of hay and crawling across the beams between them. Higher and higher I ascend towards the heavens. The further I go, the lighter I feel. I am beginning to hear myself laugh again. I run and I climb and I jump and I roll… over the hay and up the ladders and across the beams. I swing on a rope hanging down from the rafters from one mow to the next, across a great divide. Such a significant impression has been made in the hay stocks beneath me that all I can make out is darkness below. I hold my breath and don't let go… and somehow make it over to the other side without my wits failing me too substantially to prevent my succeeding.

Up, up I climb – all the way to the rafters. It's been quite a trek, yet I marvel at how I've gained the summit. I have reached its peak, and now I stand at the highest mow's outer wall looking out through the cracks between the boards. I have to brace myself against the pile of hay beside me, for my legs feel unsteady. The sensation of vertigo has my head swimming and I'm almost afraid to look down. I am so incredibly high up that everything down below looks impossibly tiny. I am so near the edge that I fear one more step could push me over. I could fall down between the boards and the mow becoming trapped there… Or worse – the boards might not hold me and I could break through and fall all the way to the ground… and to my certain death down below.

As much as the view is amazing… I can see for miles around me – across Barrett's Meadow to my home on Cabot's Hill… or if I turn my head to the east, I can see straight into town. All the fields, all the trees and landscape – I can see it all in detail.

It is so utterly breathtaking that it's almost worth the scare. No almost about it; the view alone was worth coming here – even if I have to hold onto something to do it.

Having satisfied my vision enough to turn around and begin my descent from the rafters, I receive a fright sudden enough to push me back against the fragile boards separating me from oblivion. She's standing there as clear as day in the mow entrance… It is my little friend – the one who I've lost. She is staring at me with her wide open parachute eyes. I am not sure; my senses might only be pitying me, but I can hear her giggling as though she were here and we were playing like we used to do.

CHAPTER 2

TEETERING ON THE EDGE
OF THE ABYSS

I know I'm looking at a ghost... The little girl I've loved for so long has come back to haunt me. I wondered if she would; although, I never believed it quite possible. The dead aren't supposed to come back to life. I can scarcely believe my eyes, but it is her alright – it is my Joy. It can't be but it has to be, though how can it be real? I chance the test. I close my eyes and open them again twice as quick. She's still there. I can see her face as clear as day. She's staring at me with her big blue eyes. I'm not certain of how much time passes this way. It feels like a long drawn out moment pressed into my mind, though it could just as well be an instant – shot full of buckshot and left to die in the next flash of light.

The girl does not speak. She only stares at me as though requiring my attention... Just as the thought begins to form in my head that things can't go on this way much longer, she turns as though she's about to walk away, but before leaving she raises one hand and beckons me to follow. I know I shouldn't oblige her but rather close my eyes and stay exactly where I am. I shouldn't move... I shouldn't follow... I ought to just let her go for good... In spite of the sense circling about in my head, I find myself giving in to my heartache and doing the opposite thing to reason. Like a loyal dog following its drowning master into the current, I go after the ghost.

The girl disappears down a large rectangular hay shoot swallowing up the middle of the loft. Reaching its edge, I peer over, nearly falling in in the process. The darkness sinks downward, plummeting from one hay mow to the next, down through layer upon layer of bales... before reaching God knows what below.

Teetering on the edge of the abyss, I hesitate, not sure how to proceed further. There is no ladder leading downward, just layer upon layer of baled hay... and stout, rough hone timber beams differentiating one mow from the next and breaking the monotony in silence. This is all new to me. I did not see it before. I did not come up this way. I climbed over the hay from mow to mow as though ascending one step at a time. Such giant strides took me up at least four levels – maybe more. I am very high up, that is a certainty, and the distance down is alarming. If I were to lose my balance and fall, there's a good chance I'd be done for. There is no telling what awaits me at the bottom of that pit.

I'm in the midst of considering how I should attempt my descent down the side of the mow when a sudden, shrill awareness takes hold of me that the beam I am holding onto, to steady myself, is not a beam at all but the hand of the little girl I saw disappear into the hole beneath me a moment before. A sudden burst of fear takes hold of my senses and I can feel myself losing my balance in advance of my feet beginning to give way.

I'm staring straight into her eyes, though I can't forget she's not supposed to be there. I'm as frightened as I can ever remember being, yet something prevents me from letting go.

"If you truly love me, we must do this together."

As her words varnish the insides of my eardrums with the foreboding intent of her wishes, I know it's too late to turn back. There is only one way down from here now. I stumble backwards and I stumble inward... I start to fall.

Down... down... I feel myself clawing at the dark air around me. I can't see Joy... I can't see a thing in the pitch blackness. The rushing air outside my skin is all I'm aware of... and it's sucking me in. Falling like a weight through polished lavender beneath a blanket of powdered snow, I can't imagine myself stopping. I truly feel as though I could go on this way forever... not knowing an end... not aware of the reason for my extinction. I'd just be gone for good... plummeting endlessly in the darkness... inside a barn no one knows exists. My parents might never know what happened to me. I would simply cease to exist. What a horrible way to end – one I don't wish for; although, in this unsteady moment, I can't fathom much else. How will this reach its conclusion? When I hit the bottom, I suppose – wherever that might be... It's hard to believe that there is one; I've been falling for so very long...

From one mow into the next I drop, not knowing how much time I've got before everything stops. It all seems to be about time now – how much time have I got to be without Joy... I truly thought I had more time with her. I didn't know she was going to die. I knew she was ill, but I never dreamt I would lose her. I spent three weeks by her side in her bedroom. Her parents understood our friendship and said it was alright to be there. I never went a day without visiting. I held onto her little hand and waited for her to get better so that we could go outside and play. One day became another and her health did not improve. Everyday I showed up to witness the energy being depleted further from her room. Her pulse grew a little weaker... Her eyes looked a bit more sunken in. They weren't bright anymore, and though she tried to smile, it appeared half broken. I could see her fading, but I didn't understand where it was leading. I still believed she would come back to me. I never thought I'd lose her.

On the day she died, I showed up at her house fully expecting her to be there. When her father met me at the door and handed me her white kitten, telling me to go home, I didn't understand the reason. Only afterwards, when my mother explained it to me, did I realize the meaning. In that moment my heart broke in two and something changed inside me. I haven't been the same since. I can't express my grief in accurate words or expression. My eyes are vacant, my heart derelict, left to drift out to sea to find a graveyard in the jagged years that throw themselves before me. I am still a child, yet I know so much. I know loss, I know death, I know heartache now... I know too much of what I wish not to know. I've forgotten what being a child feels like. Such crushing sorrow all at once has forced me to grow up. My enchanted season is behind me. Nothing will ever be the same again. I'm not even certain what's left of time. Darkness and fear have waged war upon my senses, yet they pale next to the deep wrenching loss inside my heart. It craves a sudden stopping at the bottom of this pit. It wants to follow that little girl straight off the end of oblivion.

CHAPTER 3

EVERYTHING AROUND ME
IS CRYSTAL DARK

It's over quickly. The landing is abrupt... but soft. I don't think I've died. If I listen closely, I believe I can still hear myself breathing. My heart is racing like a yo-yo gone wild inside my chest. It appears I've survived my ordeal. I can't make up my mind whether I'm more glad or sorry. I'm mostly glad, I think, though part of me truly didn't want to live. As sad as that sounds, I know that only one thing could change it – more time with the girl I love.

"Come; we must hurry," a voice pursues me in the dark.

I know it to be the voice of Joy, though I question how that's possible. I can't see a thing around me. Everything around me is crystal dark. I'm not sure what I landed on. The obvious conclusion would be hay, not hard packed bales but loose straw – more like chaff or bedding. If that's the case, I'm thankful someone took the time to lay this cushion down at the bottom of the vacuum that sucked me from the rafters high above me. It broke my fall so nicely that it seems too soft for stocks of hay. It feels more like the soft, moist grass that grows deep in the forest. It's funny how it smells that way too.

Without enough light reaching my eyes to

measure, I press my fingers into the layer of bedding and squeeze its flesh between them. Yes, more like grass than hay – so dense yet very much alive and breathing. I can smell the hay but it seems very far above me. It no longer feels as though I'm in a barn but rather somewhere in the woods or forest. The air is strangely fresh down here when you would think it should be stagnant.

"Come; there is no time for that," the little girl's voice reaches out of the darkness much more urgent than before.

Is it her? Is this real? I strain my eyes but I cannot see her. Only the strange scent of a newly turned forest is returned by my efforts. I raise myself on my haunches, and then to my feet. I am relieved – more surprised – to find I am unscathed from my fall. Everything still seems to work. Whatever it was I landed on, it really saved my hide. I feel as though I should go so far as to kneel down and kiss it; I truly could have died.

I can't see a thing around me; there is so little light penetrating the space I'm in. The darkness is so dense that it almost feels as though I'm completely blind. I'm beginning to worry; I hope the fall didn't damage my vision. I don't think I hit my head, but it seems so odd that I've lost all traces of light. Where could it have gone? What exactly have I fallen into?

"Come; we have no time."

All I have is the ghost girl's voice to lead

me. If it weren't for that, I truly wouldn't know which way to turn. I stumble forth blindly into the darkness that awaits, one unsteady footstep in front of the next, both arms out in front of me so as not to run into anything abrupt – and actually put my eyes out. That way I manage to gain ground, making slow progress between every one of Joy's whispered words.

"Come... this way... Hurry; we have no time."

I wonder why the urgency, though at the same time, I don't wonder at all. I know how quickly things can get lost... I know there is never enough time at all. I'm just glad to hear her voice. It's the lone beacon that guides me. It's the only lifeline I've got. I'd better cling to it as though my life depended upon it. Considering I'm as blind as a mole down a hole right now, I'm quite certain it does.

As I struggle further forth in search of a way out – in search of the thing that drew me in in the first place, I find myself nearly stumbling and falling flat on my face. At first, I blame it on the darkness or my own clumsy way, but the more I stumble the more my belief strengthens that the ground is changing beneath my feet. I am sure I'm climbing up an incline. I'm increasingly becoming aware that my unsteady efforts are taking me up somewhere. Maybe I'm climbing a hill, or perhaps I'm just climbing out of whatever it is I've fallen into.

"Come with me... Hurry," the little girl's voice, now no more than a trailing whisper, imposes doggedly upon my ears.

It's as though it's growing more distant the further I step. My progress forward is becoming more laboured, my breathing increasingly gated, hesitant, unsure of itself. Still, I keep moving onward – because, really, what other choice have I got? I can't stop and do nothing... I can't turn around.

It's almost as though it happens all of a sudden, though, truthfully, it's more of a gradual thing. I've been in the darkness for so long now I've nearly forgotten the colour of light, yet there it is – just a speck at first but gradually growing. It's the size of a knothole now and spreading wider with every tenuous step.

I can see the ground I'm walking on. It definitely does not appear as though I'm inside a barn. There looks to be sand beneath my feet, and I can see how steep the slope is that I'm climbing up. As the light ahead of me increases, I'm aware it's been a while since I last heard Joy's voice instruct. I stop and listen closely... No, not even a whisper now – only silence, like the days that followed my little friend's death. At least I can see where I'm going now. I can find my way out of this dark place. Inside my senses, I'm beginning to wonder whether her purpose here has only been to guide me. Perhaps I didn't see her up in the hay mow at the top of the barn at all. I might have simply imagined it and fallen down the chute for no more reason than my own clumsy accord. If her sole purpose was to lead me back into the light, I am grateful. I am thankful for her being here in any form at all – real or imagined. It doesn't matter; I will take it in any form at all. It has served its purpose either way.

I burst out into the open air of daylight, and it is as blinding as the pitch blackness I've left behind. I have to blink my eyes and rub them. I have to give them time to heal to the sudden change. With my vision rapidly returning, I see that now I really am in the woods. Looking behind me, I realize I have just come up out of a large hole in the ground... like some sort of rodent... like a groundhog, chipmunk or some sort of badgered coon. I'm suddenly aware of the strangest sensation. I seem out of place within my new surroundings. Everything appears to be so big... except for me, that is. I feel so tiny... compared to all the grass and trees... and the distance to the sky above me.

The earth crusted roots spread their venom around the edges of the cavern as though they wish to entangle whatever animal is bold enough to cross under their guard. They appear to be growing even as I watch them now, reaching further into the centre of the hole. I can picture them snatching me up by my collar and letting me dangle there helplessly until the ravens show up to pick the flesh off my bones. No, I think I will avoid that place entirely. I have no intention of going back in there. I will just have to find another way home.

I turn to face the forest. Another look at my surroundings should surely put things right. I must be experiencing some sort of reversed vertigo from being stuck in the dark below ground for so long. Surely that is why everything seems to be out of proportion. I close my eyes and reopen them again, just to increase my chances of seeing something different... No luck; I'm not sure what the reason is, but everything around me seems so out of scale. Have I shrunk – or has everything else grown to ten times their regular size? I don't mean to complain, but I can barely see above the blades of grass – and the trees look like skyscrapers! I wonder if I am dreaming. The fall from the haymow might have knocked me unconscious. Maybe I'm dead and have now entered the afterlife... I don't feel dead – whatever that's supposed to feel like. I guess I wouldn't know, but I couldn't imagine it feeling like this. My legs are tired from the trek up out of that hole, and if I pinch myself, it still hurts. Not to mention, my aching heart has not subdued even a little. I'm missing Joy more than ever. Where did she go? Looking around me, I don't see her anywhere, and I can't hear her voice any longer – not even a whisper on the wind. It's as though all sense of her presence has evaporated in the fragile rays of the sun streaming down through the wall of foliage in the distant treetops... its warmth breaking gently upon my skin... its touch reminding me I'm too   much   alone.

CHAPTER 4

LARGE SABRE-TOOTHED CATS ROAMING THE FOREST

"What is this – a mouse in the grass?!" a loud, pounding voice rattles my eardrums. "You should be careful, little mouse; if the wrong sort of cat comes along, you could wind up as lunch!"

As those words come bounding towards me, the large head of a cat rises out of the tall grass in front of me. It is enormous and completely white, with the pinkest pair of eyes that I've ever seen. Standing up on its haunches, I can see that it must be at least twelve feet tall. What has happened to me – or better yet, what has happened to the world around me? Nothing in this place I've fallen into is as it was or is supposed to be. I haven't got a clue where I've gone to. How can a cat grow so large – and even more absurd, how can it speak?! I scarcely know what to believe... or think... or do next. Am I merely hallucinating all this, or am I in real danger?

As the giant white feline leans in close to sniff me, I find myself more akin with the latter sentiment. That thing really could eat me! The big cat wiggles its whiskers while I stand here frozen in place and struck dumb by terror. I'm hoping I only imagined he spoke. No luck; more words spill out of its lopsided mouth as it wets its lips.

"Don't worry; you do not tempt me. I posses more discerning taste than that – and besides, I prefer my meat cooked, not raw, so you're entirely safe for the moment."

"For the moment!" I choke, with the thought oddly absent from my mind that I'm insane to be conversing with a cat.

The pale animal presses its lips into a wide grin.

"You're safe with me, period. I am here to help you. It is my duty to assist whoever passes through that gate." The sleek creature motions towards the hole in the ground I just came out of.

"That is a gate?" I feel fit to question.

"Yes, it's one of the gateways into our world."

Another question that begs an answer.

"Your world? Where exactly are we?"

"The land of the forest. It is called that because all of the land is covered with trees."

Looking around me, I see no reason to doubt what the creature says. We appear to be buried very deep in the woods, indeed. I decide to ask the next logical question that springs to mind.

"Are there any humans here – I mean creatures like me?"

The large white feline wiggles its whiskers and turns up its nose.

"None that are native to this world; however, you are not the first to come through our gates."

Somehow, I gain relief from that insight.

"You mean there have been others?"

"Oh yes, we see your kind quite regularly. Our worlds lie parallel to one another. That is why we have guardsmen like me to guide you home."

More encouragement.

"You will show me how to get back then?"

"I will assist you in finding your own way, and I will help you survive while you're here."

At this point, the big cat stretches its mouth into a frown.

"Without such assistance, it is unlikely that you would ever make it out of here alive. There are too many dangers that could befall your kind. Not everyone here is as friendly as I am. There are those who would eat you."

Talk about making a guy feel unwelcome. I don't like the sound of that.

"Is everyone here like you?" I ask, picturing large sabre-toothed cats roaming the forest.

"No, there are many different creatures living here."

"Do all the animals talk?" I'm curious to know.

"That's a silly question. How else would we communicate?"

"I don't know," I shrug, basking in the awkward silence that follows.

A long stretch of staring uncomfortably at one another proves to be accomplishing little, so I decide to break the impasse with another question.

"Do you have a name?"

Immediately my fur covered companion perks up with enthusiasm.

"Forgive me my manners. Of course I do. The name's Jackson – Jackson Trigg. I'm pleased to make your acquaintance."

It's funny how he seems to be much more pleased now than before, though I won't discourage his rejuvenated spirit, and I'm trying to accept the idea completely that I'm no longer in a place where anything I know applies. In this world, cats talk – as do other animals, apparently, so I had better do my best to listen if I ever hope to get back home, though that is not the reason I came here. I mustn't forget I was trying to find something I had lost.

"Did you happen to see a little girl come out

of the hole ahead of me?" I blurt out rather than indulge in the expected formalities of making his acquaintance.

Up to now, I couldn't even be sure he was a tom; although, I have to admit I was leaning in that direction, based on a certain degree of obvious masculinity in his voice.

Jackson Trigg looks dumbfounded.

"There was no one else, only you."

I shake my head in disbelief.

"But that's not possible... I followed her here. She led me out of the hole in the ground."

The large cat smiles sympathetically.

"I'm sorry, but I didn't see anyone else – and I never take my eyes off that gate. There is no way anyone could have slipped by me without me noticing."

I don't think it wise to suggest he might have been sleeping. I still don't entirely trust that he won't eat me... I am yet to trust that what I'm experiencing is real. The odds are becoming remarkably more favourable that this is the direct result of hitting my head.

I can't believe that he didn't see her; although, when I think on it steady, I barely saw her myself. And I haven't seen her at all since my fall. Perhaps I only imagined hearing her voice.

Regardless, without Joy here, as intriguing as this place appears to be, all I truly want to do is go home.

"How do I get home?" I ask boldly.

The fat cat smiles before half purring out his answer.

"Simple, you have to find what you came here in search of. Once you find that, you will find your way home."

"What?!" I exclaim. "What happens if I don't find it? Will I be stuck here?"

The large white cat called Jackson Trigg does not answer. In fact, he goes so far as to look away, as though afraid to make eye contact.

"Will I be stuck here?!" I raise my voice to a yell this time.

"No human ever stays here for long," he almost whispers.

Somehow, that is not very reassuring.

"What do you mean? What happens to them?"

"They either find what they're looking for or they don't."

"And if they don't, what then?" I beg to know.

"Then they are lost..."

"Lost! You mean they die?!" I gasp.

Jackson nods.

"Or something worse. There are many dangers here. This world is not a safe place for humans."

"But I thought you were supposed to help me!" I entreat.

"I am helping you. It is my duty... It is the way."

"Then how can I be lost?"

The cat shrugs.

"That part is up to you. Some don't want to find what they came in search of."

He looks at me seriously.

"What did you come here to find?"

"I came here to find my friend."

Jackson Trigg shakes his head.

"She's not here."

"But I followed her here. I need to find her." I plead.

The cat shakes its head with more

conviction than before.

"I'm sorry but your little friend isn't here. What is it that you really want?"

He's right; I know she can't be... I know she's not here anymore. I watched her be buried up on Cabot's Hill. I know what I saw – if I saw her at all – was a ghost. I don't know why I saw her or why she has led me here, but I do know that she's the reason I'm here – wherever that is. If it's anything more than a dream, I can't be certain. I've never seen anything like it, yet it feels very real... in spite of talking cats and mammoth vegetation.

I look over my shoulder to see a daisy bending down to greet me – with a head the size of a wagon wheel. It's orange and brown and yellow and gold and very imposing. It shakes and quivers under its own frequency. I half expect it to speak, though it doesn't appear to have that ability. I think it just as well; I'm not sure how I would handle more strangeness.

"In your world, do all the animals speak the way you do?" I feel fit to question more directly.

"Only those of us who need to. Everything communicates in its own way, of course. You might not be able to understand the plants or the trees, but they are speaking too. But for those of us who must, we do – but that is entirely for your benefit. It's not on our own account, that you can be certain. I am here to guide you, so guide you I shall. I will ask you again. What is it that you really want?"

"More time!" I blurt out without thinking.

The white cat looks confused.

"More time... you say?"

"Yes, more time with my friend Joy. She left too soon. I didn't think she was going to die. I didn't have a chance to say goodbye. She wasn't supposed to go. We were supposed to have a lifetime together."

Jackson looks sympathetic.

"I am sorry. I know it's not easy to lose someone you're close to."

"It's not fair. I loved her. I need more time with her... I'm just asking for a little more time, that's all."

The large cat is solemn and unwavering in tone.

"I'm sorry, but I can't help you. There is no time here."

I don't understand.

"But there has to be. Don't you have seasons? Doesn't the sun rise in the morning and set at night? Were you not born and do you not grow old? Your world must have a concept of time. How can it not?"

Jackson shakes his head diligently.

"Everything is just as it's always been, entering into and leaving the moment as it happens. There is no night. We do not age. We are either here or we're not. Everything is here until it is not. We all exist until we do not. There is no time to give."

"I need more time with Joy," I beg.

The imposing feline is nearly on the verge of spitting.

"I've told you; there is no time!" Jackson furiously declares.

I'm at my wit's end; I don't know what else to tell him.

"But that's why I've come here! It's what I've come in search of – so you have to help me!"

I think I've got him this time; to deny me would go against his sworn duty as a guardsman or whatever he said he is.

"I can't help you. I'm afraid you'll have to go it alone. You will have to find your own way home – or perish in the process. Either way, it's up to you now."

I couldn't have been more wrong. Now I'm in it up to my knees.

"You can't leave me by myself; I have no idea how to get home. If my friend isn't here – if I can't find her and there is no such thing as time, what am I supposed to be looking for? How will I ever find my way out of here?!"

Jackson Trigg turns the other way and begins to walk off before stopping to impart some more wisdom.

"I am sorry, but I cannot help you with your request. You should have chosen wiser. You should have known better than to ask for too much. Now you are all alone."

With that, the giant cat bounds away. In three long strides, he is gone into the trees, to be seen no more. Before long, even the sound of his large paws flattening the moss on the forest floor gets swallowed up by the silence. Now it's only me and the wind in the woods keeping company – and the wind isn't much of a listener. It whines way too much to hear what I'm saying... Joy was a good listener – she was the best, but she's not here anymore.   I   truly   am   all   alone.

CHAPTER 5

CHASING A GIANT JACKRABBIT THROUGH THE WOODS

It's hard to believe that what just happened happened. Part of me wants to believe I was imagining that too – just like everything else in this place, but the largest part of me wishes the big white cat were still here and willing to help me... as imposing as he came across... as threatening as he first seemed. I was growing more accustomed to his company the longer he paced about, even though he could have grabbed me by the scruff of my neck and shaken me to death at any given moment or fallen me with one swift swipe of his massive paws.

Amidst my fear and growing worries, a sense of hunger washes over me. In spite of the sky lacking a sunset to predict the lateness of the hour, I'm certain it's well after supper. I'm feeling lightheaded and my stomach is starting to growl. My rational mind is telling me I should have asked the white cat to help me with something more practical than finding a ghost. I should have asked him to feed me. However, I felt I had to be honest. What is the point of being here if I'm not? If this is real... if there is a purpose to anything. Regardless, I could sure use something to eat.

I look to the path that Jackson fled. I look behind me. I can't go back; the hole I came out of isn't there anymore. It has disappeared. I look around me. It doesn't matter which way I go; it all looks the same to me.

Just as I'm about to choose which direction to set out in, I'm struck on my back by a force sufficient enough to knock me to my knees. A loud sniffing sound in my ears is accompanied by a soft, moist sensation on the back of my neck. I'm afraid to turn around to see what new horror awaits me. I want to just stay where I am with my eyes sealed tight, but I know I must turn and face the potential danger. I can't just lie down and play dead; I could wind up on someone's dinner plate that way.

I muster enough courage to peer over my shoulder... A giant sniffling rabbit's nose slaps a sloppy wet kiss against my face, knocking me back onto the seat of my pants. Attached to the sopping sniffer is the elongated head and body of the largest grey and brown jack rabbit I've ever seen. As it sniffs me rapidly in a hyper – almost aggressive – manner, I am acutely aware that its two massive front teeth look strong – and sharp – enough to bite my head off!

"What are you?!" the jack rabbit demands to know.

I'm amused by how the creature used *what* rather than *who*. However, as I'm not so severely shocked as I was upon first seeing the white cat, I'm able to formulate a quicker response this time around.

"My name is Forrester. I'm a boy from the other world. I came through one of the gates in the ground."

"Hmph!" the sabre-toothed jackrabbit snorts. "You don't smell like carrots."

I'm thinking that's a good thing. If it had turned out to be to the contrary, I wouldn't be liking my chances one little bit.

"That's because I'm not food. I'm a human."

"I've heard of your kind but have only seen one once before – and he was food! The swamp-fish were picking the flesh off his bones."

I don't like the sound of that.

"Swamp-fish! What are they?"

"Great schools of them live in the cold water swamps that wind through these woods. They're half the size of me but with teeth like razors. You'd be best to steer clear of the bogs or you'll wind up like the other one."

Some more of the danger that Jackson Trigg warned about, I imagine.

"Are there any around here?" I deem necessary to know.

He points his nose in one direction.

"Just through those trees a whippet's wail and over a rise. If you go in that direction, you can't miss them, but I wouldn't recommend you going that way. In fact, I go out of my way to avoid it."

"Why? Do they eat rabbits too?"

The big grey and brown creature actually looks scared.

"They eat anything that is unfortunate enough to fall into the water."

I make up my mind without hesitation. Nope, I don't think I'll travel in that direction – and I won't be cooling my toes in any bubbling brooks.

The large rabbit appears to be growing impatient.

"Anyways, my name is Pilache. I'm on my way to the berry patch. You're welcome to tag along."

With that, he hops away in a dash, and I make up my mind to follow him. If I want to eat, I figure this is my best chance. I know I don't have much time before he disappears from view, so I hurry down the path after his fluffy tail.

When I got out of bed this morning, if I thought I'd be chasing a giant jackrabbit through the woods, I would have believed myself certifiably insane, yet here I am doing it anyways. I don't know how to feel about that.

It's all I can do to keep up with him. I'm winded and weary and lathered in a thick layer of sweat by the time the bounding creature slows to something resembling a standstill. As I get beyond a dense thicket and make my way over a slight rise, I see what all the fuss is about. In a small clearing beneath a nest of large tree trunks lies the most peculiar berry patch that I've ever come across. Between a massive tangle of vines are hundreds of gigantic plum coloured fruit. They are shaped like strawberries but without the speckling of seeds covering their skin. I now see that we are not alone. Another five jackrabbits are already dug in and feasting upon the berries' plump flesh. They're so engrossed in their efforts that they hardly seem bothered enough by my arrival to acknowledge my presence. Granted, it would be difficult for some, seeing that each has its entire head buried inside a berry's hull. One snow white creature pulls back to reveal a completely purple head. Upon seeing me, all it does is wiggle its whiskers in a disinterested fashion before resuming its pleasant work. My friend, whose heels I came in on, wastes no time in setting up shop beside a particularly juicy looking morsel and proceeds to dig in.

Between its first foray of mouthfuls, the creature turns to me and offers, "Feel free to help yourself. There is more than enough to go around."

That I have no doubt of. There looks to be enough fruit in the berry patch to feed a hundred giant jackrabbits – and a thirteen year old boy, to boot! Before his head disappears back into the juicy sack, rendering it near impossible to hear me, I beg to know one more thing.

"What are these berries called?"

I'm not sure if Pilache heard me at first; there is no response from inside the berry's shell, but eventually the binging rabbit takes a breath long enough to get out the muffled words, "Claw-hawk berries."

What an odd name to give a berry, I think to myself. It doesn't sound nearly as nice as blue or straw or even thimble berry.

"Why are they called that?" I risk asking.

Again a delay... and again a surprise answer.

"Because claw-hawks love to feed off them."

"Claw-hawks!" I choke. "What are those?!"

The rabbit is no longer hiding its head inside its dinner, but rather, is fully engaged in our conversation.

"They are big black birds with sharp claws for ripping apart their food. They fly in large flocks that range across the sky for as far as the eye can see."

"Are berries all they eat?" I ask hopefully.

The way the rabbit shakes its head gives

away the answer before any words are spoken.

"They eat everything! If you ever see one, run!"

Suddenly I feel very much like a mouse at the bait. I can't help but think that it's only a matter of time before something terrible happens. I don't have a good feeling about this. The only thing keeping me from making myself scarce right this present moment is the gnawing hole in my gut. If I don't eat something soon, I fear I'll become too faint to continue and collapse on the ground. I would be vulnerable to claw-hawks – or anything at that point, so I decide it best not to tempt fate and miss out on this chance at feeding, for who knows when or where my next meal will be.

Cautiously searching the sky with my eyes before proceeding, I summon the courage necessary to go forth. Taking a deep breath, content enough in my head that we're not about to be pillaged from above, I make my way down to one of the large plum, sweet smelling fruit along the edge of the patch.

At such close range, I realize that its aroma is indeed very sweet – almost like lavender and lilac with a hint of licorice thrown in for adventure. I reach into its soft flesh and pull loose a handful of supple fruit. I sniff it closely and it does smell delicious. I can't help but taste it now. I place a small piece in my mouth and slowly begin to chew... It's not long before I swallow and am taking another bite. It is delicious. No wonder the rabbits risk coming here. The claw-hawk berry deserves a much better name. The one given does not do it justice. I reach in and take another handful. I can't get enough of the scrumptious fruit. I find myself eating more and more.

I'm enjoying myself so intensely that I somehow manage to lose track of time, worry and all things in between. I'm not sure how much I've consumed, but judging by the large hole I've carved in the side of the berry, I'd guesstimate somewhere around a quarter of my body weight. Honestly, I had no idea that my stomach could hold so much.

Neither I nor the rabbits seem to be paying much attention to anything outside the pleasant act of gorging ourselves. If we were, we might have seen it coming. By the time we do, it's almost too late. I'm not exactly sure what caused me to look up. Maybe it was a sense that things had been just a little too calm for a little too long. Perhaps I heard something that I don't remember hearing. Whatever it was, it urged me to look up towards the heavens... Between the leaf covered branches on the trees, in the space of sky that would regularly be blue, all I see is black. Everything is covered in it, like tar paper spread across a canvas, like oil blocking out the sun, for as far as I go on looking, for as distant as my naked eye can see, an uneasy darkness inhabits the land.

"What is that?!" I find myself yelling.

The tone of my voice appears frantic enough for all six rabbits to listen. There is not one that doesn't look up. Moreover, they're all standing to attention, upright on their haunches, whiskers twitching, with their ears pointing to no end.

"Claw-hawks!" the rabbits all cry together.

Look where our distraction has led us. A sick feeling is descending upon me – faster than the darkness coming down from the sky. Will this be my ruin? Is this how my life will end? Will I be reunited with my friend sooner than I thought?

There is clearly no time to waste. Faster than I thought possible for a four hundred pound animal to move, one frantic rabbit after another races off into the dense cover of the forest. There is not another word – no warning for me to follow. I am left alone to fend for myself. Where's Jackson Trigg when I need him?

With ear splitting velocity, a thousand cries rain down from above.

"Caw... caw..." the shrill daggers stab at my eardrums. I can hear a whooshing in the trees and feel the pressure of a newly generated wind. I'm almost certain of it now. I know there is no time to run.

CHAPTER 6

SOMETHING MOVING IN THE SHADOWS

As the last remaining light surrounding me gets doused out and black feathers and razor claws are near enough to scratch my skin, something tells me to take a step back. I act without thought, question or doubt. I just do it, and for whatever reason, it proves my salvation. No sooner do I move my feet does the ground open up beneath me and pull me in. The firm earth gives way and I get sucked down into its gizzards – just fast enough to escape dozens of razor sharp talons. I'm certain one caught hold of my hair. Before going under, I had just enough time to catch a glimpse of one of the birds of prey. As large as a rhino, as black as a fully eclipsed sun, with bloodshot eyes and a viciously curved beak – more closely resembling a reaping hook than anything natural belonging to a bird. If I'd stood there one instant longer, I would have surely been torn to ribbons by that thing... If I'd stood there one second longer, I'd be pinned to the ground by those gigantic claws right now, with one of them riveted through my skull. I hope all the rabbits made it to safety. I'd hate to imagine it any other way.

This time, my fall is short lived. I have little time to think about it because it is over in a hurry. Within mere seconds of feeling the ground give way beneath me, I reach my destination. I find myself inside some underground earthen lair. I couldn't have fallen much beyond twenty feet, yet it seems plenty deep enough to be buried – and it sure beats the alternative. Oddly, it's not dark down here like a reasonable person would assume it ought to be. There's a warm light flickering in the distance casting long shadows about some sort of room. Adjusting my eyes to the dim aperture, there looks to be a fire in a hearth along the far wall. There is a large pot hung on a rod above the flames, and I can hear bubbling and smell some sort of soup cooking. Its odour comes across as appealing – much like something my grandmother would make... when I was a little younger... and she was still alive.

What's this?! I see something moving in the shadows. It appears to be half the size of the room! It is a large creature – like everything else around this godforsaken place! Before I can even consider making it to my feet, the beast is upon me and sniffing me all over.

"What's this? What's this?" with a few more sniffs in between. "Who are you? And what are you doing in my home?"

All reasonable questions – and all very deserving of answers.

"I am Forrester. I am a boy. I was in the berry patch up above with a colony of rabbits when we were attacked by a murder of crows... aw, I mean, Claw-hawks, I guess. Thankfully, the ground gave way beneath me before they got hold of me. It was a very close call. I really thought I was a goner."

The creature nods its head in a sympathetic manner.

"Those birds are relentless. That is why I stay down here. I only go up to the surface when I have to, and it's usually under cover of night. All the animals are afraid of them. When they're on the hunt, no one is safe."

"I'm not from around here, but I got the just of that pretty quickly as soon as I laid eyes on them. I didn't mean to invade your privacy; falling down here was an accident."

The large animal shakes its head from side to side.

"Think nothing of it. You've made a bit of a mess that I will have to tidy up, but it's a good thing you fell when you did. If they'd gotten hold of you, you would have been a goner. But we don't want to think about that now, do we? No, no we don't, so we won't. We'll content ourselves with having some soup."

Encouraged by his ease of candour, I do some asking of my own.

"Who are you?"

"Oh, I'm sorry; I thought that much was

obvious. I'm a mole, of course. I burrow in the ground and make tunnels underneath the earth. Couldn't you tell by my snout?"

"I can't tell what you look like; it's too dark down here."

The mole shuffles over to the hearth.

"Forgive me; I forget sometimes. Let me give you more light. I don't require it myself; I work best in the dark."

From out of the shadows, the creature produces a torch. He ignites it in the flames of the fire, before carrying it over and placing it near me to illuminate the room.

"My name is Marik. I am a keeper of the space beneath the ground. I tend to the foundation of the surface world – that which everything is built upon."

Lit by the torch, I can see that the mole is dark grey with a long snout and great folds of skin rolling down his belly. He plops his large bottom down a few feet away from me on a bed made out of moss, grass and leaves.

"Phew! Sometimes just moving around my den can be exhausting. Pardon me, but I need to rest for a while before we can be on our way. First we will share a bowl of leek soup in front of the fire."

The stout mole motions towards the hearth.

"There are bowls and a ladle on the mantel. If you don't mind helping yourself, you can fill a bowl for me in the process."

As I get to my feet, I dust the dirt off my bottom and make a more detailed study of my surroundings. Several stacks of dried grass and open bins containing various vegetables such as corn, squash, carrots, potatoes, leeks and beans line the earthen walls of the room. Other than food and bedding, the space lies mostly empty. I can see that the rest of the square footage needs to be dedicated to the safe movement of the friendly mole himself. A cluttered compartment would not serve someone of his bulk well. I wonder how he fares in the tunnels.

Thinking it best to approach the subject delicately, I inquire, "Do you do much tunnelling down here?"

The mole contemplates his answer as he watches me make my way over to the fireplace to begin the process of ladling out the soup.

"A fair bit, but it's tiresome work. I must admit; it gets to me sometimes and I just want to rest in my den. All that moving of earth, the constant digging... It's an endless pursuit. Nevertheless, it's what I do."

The staunch fellow perks up at this point.

"We all have our talents and we must make use of them. We were not given our gifts to waste, after all. With that said, you will come with me after we've had our soup. You will follow me deeper into the ground."

"Where are we going?" I ask hesitantly.

"I will show you why you are here. I will take you to what you've been searching for."

I can scarcely believe my ears.

"How do you know what I'm searching for?" I ask rather defensively.

The mole looks at me as though I've just asked the most ridiculous question in the world.

"Because I've seen her down here."

I go further.

"Who?"

"The little girl... The one who is called Joy."

Could it be true? I want to believe that it is. If it weren't, how could the mole know her name?

"You've seen her?!" I risk questioning what has already been stated.

"Yes, I've been seeing her for weeks now. At first, I could only hear her in the distance – down in the tunnels, but eventually, she took form."

I'm not sure what to think about all this.

"Did she say anything else, other than her name?" I need to know.

The mole nods his head.

"Yes, she said a boy would be coming in search of her. For weeks now, every night I've gone down into the tunnels – and every night I've seen her, but only in the distance and only for a fleeting moment at a time, way down the tunnel ahead of me. She always delivers the exact same message – that a boy would be coming for her."

I truly don't know what to think. Though it's the very thing I've been yearning for... the very thing I've been desperately wanting to hear, I can't help having my doubts.

"How were you able to see her? I thought moles are supposed to be blind."

The big fat rodent looks less than pleased.

"That, I'll have you know, is a gross embellishment of the truth! Our eyesight might be limited due to the amount of time we spend below ground in the dark, but we are far from blind!"

I apologize emphatically.

"I'm sorry; I didn't realize..."

"No bother," the wrinkly creature dismisses. "The important thing is that you are here. Before you turned up, I thought I was losing my mind. If I'm not seeing the girl down in the tunnels, I'm dreaming about her at night and resurrecting her in my thoughts by day. Even before she started appearing to me, I could hear her voice in my head... and down deep in the tunnels... for days before I actually saw her. Now that you are here, I'm hoping it will stop. The message has always been for you. I am only the conduit. I am only supposed to take you to her."

"She is the reason that I'm here. I followed her down here. I am trying to find her. I need more time with her."

The very wise looking mole nods.

"She clearly brought you here for a reason, but if it's time you're looking for, you won't find it here."

"I don't understand... Then why did she bring me here? It's all I want."

"It is not for us to understand. I am to take you to her, that is all. The rest is up to you."

Clutching the wooden bowl in both paws, the mole empties its remnants into his mouth.

"We had best be on our way. She'll be waiting for us."

It takes the bulky creature a couple of tries to roll onto his stomach in order to push off the ground enough to raise himself. Once back on all fours, the winded mole needs a moment to catch his breath before continuing.

"Phew!" he gasps. "That was hard work. I really must lose some weight. Too much soup... too much soup."

He clutches his robust belly and laughs.

"I have to work twice as hard as I should – digging extra wide tunnels so that I don't get stuck. But it's no bother; I like my soup too well."

I'm just glad he didn't roll on top of me by accident while in the awkward process of rousing himself to his feet. I have to giggle to myself; it was quite comical to watch.

"Come now, follow me closely. I don't want you getting left behind in the dark or you will become lost. The tunnels are too narrow for me to turn around, so it will take forever to find you again."

I swig my own bowl of soup back and obey. I've been down here in the dark enough already. I have no desire for that pattern to persist.

"May I bring the torch along?" I ask hopefully.

"Sorry, but no; the firelight would interfere with my own sense of direction. I can navigate much better without it. However, to do things safely, I suggest that you grab hold of my tail. That way, I shouldn't lose you in the dark."

I grab hold of the stout stub and we are off. Moving quickly along behind the creature's wiggling rump, it's all I can do to keep up. As he moves, his rear end wiggles, and as it wiggles, his tail wiggles – and I wiggle right along with it. We wind our way down deep into the ground. The further we go – with every scurrying, pulling motion, the more claustrophobic I become. If it wasn't for the sake of finding Joy, I would pass on such an unsettling experience entirely and choose to stay above ground; although, I fear I'm too hastily forgetting my reasons for going underground. Staying on the surface would have been no less unsettling. In fact, I'm all but certain it would have meant the death of me. The image of those ugly black birds descending upon me and ripping me apart with their talons suddenly disrupts my balance and I find myself stumbling out of control. I lose my grip on Marik's tail and wind up flat on my face in the moist black dirt.

"Ugh! Wait!" I bleat out in panic like some half bloated sheep.

Mercifully, my tunnel guide hears my gurgled words – or else, feels my pressure absent from his tail... or both, and slams on the brakes.

"What's that? Where did you go, little fella?" I can hear greasing the walls of the tunnel back in my direction.

"I tripped... Give me a moment so that I can find you in the dark and grab hold of you again."

I hear laughter trickling back towards me now.

"I can't give you a moment, but I can wait until you find me. I will whistle while I wait, and it will help guide you."

The mole's whistling – though I'm sure intended to be cheerful, finds its way back to me in the most haunting, mournful way possible. It's the saddest cry upon the wind that I have ever heard uttered. It sweeps the earth's walls in bitter lament, howling as it winds by me, passes and grows distant. It nearly brings me to tears as I think of all I've lost... the one who I was closest to... She was dearer to me than my own parents. Though they are not bad people and I believe they love me... they are nothing near to what I had in Joy. Two souls could not have been closer. Our years spent together cannot be undone – and are impossible to forget... Playing together everyday... sharing our hopes and our dreams... our fears and our doubts... comforting each other when we were afraid... planning for a future that never came to pass... seeing each other change and embracing that change... knowing that each day the sun chose to rise we would be there as constant as the grass is green in summer... knowing we would always be there for each other, no matter what... through thick and thin, though come what may... We shared a love so pure that it wasn't meant to end. We were destined for a life together – a life so full and grand that I can't help mourning such a grievous loss. Who had the right to take it all away? Who had the right to ruin my life and leave me empty? We were going to be married one day... and have a family. We were going to be so happy... We were so happy! We basked in the splendour of life every single day. Who had the right to bring that to an end?! I feel robbed and betrayed by God or someone... by life maybe... I need something to blame. I know I had it all... and now it feels as though I have nothing.

Aided by his whistling, I find my friend the mole in the dark and place one hand on his tail. Once again we begin our steady descent into the ground. It seems odd to me that I can still hear Marik whistling – even though it's for no obvious purpose, yet I don't say a thing. I just continue to follow. There's no sense in impeding our progress.

As we move along, I'm beginning to doubt whether the mole is making the sound at all. It seems to be originating somewhere further ahead... and it's not so much a whistling but more of a whine. The more we slip underground, the more the shrill echo resembles my name.

"Forrester... Forrester..."

I am now certain it's a voice – not any voice but the voice of a young girl... the voice of Joy. I have no doubts left in my head. She is down here somewhere, and she's calling out my name. Chills are running up and down my spine. I don't know if I'm ready for this. Even though Marik is with me, I don't know what to expect. How can she be anything more than a ghost? I watched her be buried no more than four weeks ago tomorrow.

I can feel my companion slowing in front of me.

"This is as far as I can take you. You'll have to go the rest of the way alone," he states in as confident a tone as he can manage.

I am caught entirely off guard by his announcement.

"Why? What's the matter? Can you not come with me?"

"I can't; the way is too narrow."

I don't buy his explanation immediately.

"But can you not tunnel through it?"

His hesitation doesn't help improve upon my mood.

"I can, but I won't; you must do this alone. I do know that much. My role is to guide you to her. What happens after that is entirely up to you; it has to be. This is your path. These are your choices to make. It is why you've come here."

With that, my hand slips free of his tail and I hear him scurry away down a tunnel to my left, leaving these scant parting words for encouragement.

"Remember you are here for a reason, but

don't forget that what you seek does not exist."

What kind of a twisted riddle is that? Of course I'm here for a reason, and I know I'm trying to find what I've lost. But how can it not exist? I've lost Joy, and I'm only here because I followed her to this place. That fat cat, Jackson Trigg, told me she wasn't here, but the mole said differently – and he's shown me as much. I can hear her voice calling me forth. Looking up ahead, way down the tunnel, I can make out a flicker of light. I know it's her. It must   be.   What   else   could   it   be?

CHAPTER 7

A QUIET, STEADY WHISPER

The chills running up and down my spine are travelling further. The thought trespasses over my mind that what if it's not her. What if it's something else... something darker and unkind? I am suddenly feeling very alone in the dark. I can no longer hear Marik's soft pattering in the distance. He has long since abandoned me now. Down here, deep beneath the earth, my only companion is what awaits me at the end of that tunnel.

Carefully now, slowly, taking great care not to fall, I make my way along the narrow passage. It's steep enough that if I should fall, I might not be able to prevent myself from tumbling all the way down into whatever awaits me at the end of the corridor. I'm not sure why I am so afraid. You'd think I'd be glad to see Joy again... And I would be – if I knew exactly what I would be seeing... and why she is waiting for me way down here.

The hairs are standing rigid along the back of my neck and my entire body is numb with fear. My nervous mind cannot be quieted. What have I gotten myself into? I would turn around and go back right now if I thought I could find my way back through the darkness. All I've got is the dull glow up ahead to guide me. Without it, I'd be entirely in the dark – and buried God knows how deep in the earth! No, there is but one way I can go now. I just hope that what I find at the end of the road is love.

As I get closer, the revelations are starting to scratch at the wall I've built up around my senses. Fear can do a lot to a person – and grief will do even more. The light is not artificial, nor has it been generated by any other source. A little girl is standing in its midst at the end of the tunnel, which has snuck up very close while I've been distracted by my thoughts.

I force myself a few steps nearer and realize, without a grain of doubt for seeping, that the little girl is Joy. The veil of fear subsides for just a moment as I allow my heart to fill with warmth. It's really her – well, as near to life as someone dead can be... At least, as near to life as she appeared to me in the haymow at the top of the barn, though I can't even be sure that that was real... I can't cease from wondering why I never noticed the barn before.

I can't be certain whether she's real or imagined. I can't even be certain if I'm here, though I must be; I've got to be somewhere. Maybe I am dead, yet I still feel pain and fear. I am filled with emotion. My heart has opened up and allowed all the ache inside to travel forth. All I want to do is run into her arms and hold her... tell her how much I've missed her... all the things I should have said – and wanted to but never found the courage. I love this girl beyond reason... I always have – I know it.

I cannot accept that I've lost her... I cannot face another day without her in my life.

My little friend is standing there in front of me, amidst a ball of light, real enough to touch and hold, yet seemingly frozen and unreachable just as much. As I look more closely, it appears as though she's trying to move her lips to say something but her words cannot penetrate the film of light surrounding her. It's almost as though she's trapped inside it, unable to leave. Thinking back, I can't altogether recall when I stopped hearing her calling my name. Was it before Marik left me alone in the dark? Was it when fear took hold of me with a strangled embrace about my neck? I can't be certain now, though it feels like it's been a while. Everything is so quiet... like the dead calm before a storm... like inside the eye of a tornado... like anticipation.

Though I ought to be too afraid to try, I somehow force myself to do it. I reach out one unsteady hand to touch her – just to see if further senses recognize her presence here as real. My fingers quiver as they anticipate the light... but, strangely, feel as though they can go no further. It's as though there is a wall around her. As hard as I try to penetrate the barrier, I can't bring myself closer... I can't quite reach her. I'm pushing towards her with everything I've got yet going nowhere – gaining in no real way that matters. I've become stuck in the light.

Joy is trying to say something but her words

can't reach me – and I can't reach her. What a sad display of truth. Though she's standing directly in front of me, she's never been further away. Tears are welling up in my eyes and streaming down my face. I'm caught in a vicious cycle of emotional release – out of sadness... out of the relentless frustration of being so close.

What is happening? Why did she bring me here for this? This is worse than not seeing her at all. All it does is haunt me... It torments my soul. It reminds me of everything I've lost.

I pull back, becoming rigid and still, for no real reason discernible to my senses – at least, nothing obvious at first. With a little time, though, as is usually the way, my unease becomes clearer. It no longer hesitates beneath the window. It doesn't bother to linger outside the door. It is right there screaming in my ears. A voice speaks to me. It's no more than a quiet, steady whisper. It sits on my shoulders and crawls up inside my head. I know it's not Joy's voice; she's still trapped behind her veil of light. I'm not sure whether it's male or female; it is sufficiently neutral in scope. I'm not even certain I know where it's coming from. It's as though it's all around and nowhere at all at the same time. I can't even be certain it's not originating inside my own head. Although, I don't think it is, for I've never heard such a tone in all my life.

"You have come here to be with the girl, yes?"

I find myself nodding my head without thinking.

"I miss her..."

"And what is it that you would like more than anything?"

I can't believe I'm hearing this voice, nor can I be certain of where it's coming from. I'm down in a dark narrow tunnel, several levels below ground, all alone with a frozen ghost and a mysterious disembodied voice. I should be over the top afraid. I ought to be running for my life in the other direction, yet I'm standing my ground and praying I'll be given what I ask for.

"I want more time... I need more time with her – that's all I ask. I want a life with her. Can you give me that?"

There is no pause – only an answer.

"There is no time here. I can't give you what doesn't exist."

"Then, what has brought me here? Why can't she talk to me? Why is she trapped in the light like that?" I demand to know.

Again, there is no hesitation – only direct, obligatory response.

"Your desire brought you here – yours and hers both. She can't interact with you because she's not really here."

"Am I really here?!" I nearly shout.

"Where else would you be?" the voice challenges.

"I don't know – dreaming maybe... For all I know, I could be dead."

"Does this place not seem real to you?" the voice continues.

"Yes, it does... and I don't remember falling asleep or being knocked unconscious – or dying, for that matter."

I can almost discern a hint of a chuckle in the tone.

"Then it must be very real. Would you not agree?"

"Well, yes, but she seems just as real, and if she's not really here, then maybe I'm not either."

"But you are here, for we just determined that you could be no other place – and you are here because you believe her to be."

Now I'm really getting confused.

"Well, yes, but what does that have to do with anything?"

"It has everything to do with it all. It is why you are here. You seek more time with your friend, but she has no more time. She's not really here because everything here takes place in the moment, for there is no time here at all."

I'm having a hard time comprehending what this is all about.

"What do you mean?! Where is she then?! She seems so real. I can almost reach out and touch her."

The voice doesn't waiver in tone or intent.

"She no longer lives in the moment – only in the future or in the past. What you've seen up until now has been part of the past."

I'm trying my best to understand.

"But how can she have a future if she doesn't have a present?"

"Because she no longer has a present, she will never get to live in the future, that is a given, yet it's still there to see as it might have been. However, you can only see it if you are viewing it from the right vantage point."

"And where is that?" I beg to know.

"It's only possible to view the future from a place where time does not exist."

Finally, something that holds some promise.

"So I can see it from here?"

"Yes, but remember, it is a future that will

never be – only what could have been. It is possible to see it – even experience it from here – but not actually live it, for it can never be."

"I don't understand. What do you mean?"

"It is possible for you to feel as though you are there with her in the future. It will seem very real, for it is the life you could have had. However, it will be a sped up version. You will only experience certain events or specific moments – like a highlight reel, if you will. It will only last for a short duration and then it will be over. But I must warn you; you can only view it once – but never again... and it might not be entirely what you were expecting or hoping for. You run the risk of seeing things that will leave you feeling worse – with a greater sense of loss than you have at present... You might see things that you don't want to see."

In spite of the dire warnings, I am feeling a new sense of hope.

"You mean that it is possible for me to be with her again?"

"In a manner of speaking, yes. But I must warn you; it does not come without a cost."

"What is it? I'll do anything!" I insist.

"For a glimpse of a future that will never be, you must give up part of yours that hasn't happened yet. Only then will you be allowed to view the one that's lost."

I don't want to hesitate or think about it any longer. I want to scream out, *I will do anything! I don't care about any other future! I don't want a future without Joy in it!* However, I refrain for long enough to contemplate the dilemma presented my way, for I really should think about things a while before committing to such stringent terms. What exactly would I be giving up? I must make sure that I comprehend it fully... that I'm comfortable with trading away pieces of my life. My reasonable self tells me I might regret this decision someday, but another part just as sensible says it doesn't matter; I will never know what I'd be giving up anyways – and my heart trumps it all by insisting that one more day with Joy would be worth anything... I would give up anything... I have no doubt in my mind, heart or soul... I truly love her.

"Yes, I will do it. I will give up whatever I have to."

If ever I've sensed hesitation in my words, it is now.

"Yes," I answer without delay.

"Are you certain? You must understand that once done it cannot be reversed."

I nod.

"I understand."

"Then, let it be done. It is your choice to make. It is why you have come here."

With that, the voice is gone, sucked into the vacuum of darkness. For the first time, I feel as though I am truly alone with Joy – the way it used to be when it was just the two of us caught in the silence of a wayward afternoon... underneath a maple tree on a swing... or walking along some quiet country lane.

CHAPTER 8

THE MOST BEAUTIFUL LIFE

The light surrounding Joy seems to have changed. I can hear her now, and she's reaching out to touch my hand.

"Forrester, I've missed you. I've been waiting for you here."

Her words caress the inside of my heart, like honey being spread over a warm bun.

"I've missed you too... I've missed you too..." I emphasize with all of my might as I throw my arms around her in a longing embrace.

"I've come for you. I've followed you here, just like you wanted me to."

The sweet little girl with an unmistakable twinkle once more in her eye nods to me slowly.

"I knew you would... if I asked you to."

We both knew I would. I don't think there was ever any question.

Still holding onto each other tightly, somehow more intimately than ever before, we look into each other's eyes – and we're gone down the tunnel in a flash... the light around us acting as a shield against all that would harm us... carrying us over every proverbial bump in the road. The darkness has parted ways with our company. It's had no choice; it, like everything else now, revolves around us.

The deeper underground we go, the more I'm becoming aware of the true nature of our surroundings. Everything is shifting in a continuous rhythm, like waves rolling over us and folding us in. Light is flooding into the tunnel and space is opening up in every direction. We are no longer in a tunnel but on some sort of vast plain with no walls or borders at all. It's as though boundaries are not present – or at least, have not bothered to make the effort to exist.

Suddenly – with a jolt, as though we've been shaken awake, we are sent tumbling into a meadow. It's familiar to us both. We've been here often over the course of years. We know this place intimately. It lies just two rests short of Cabot's Hill before the land rises to meet the forest. It has been a most worthy companion to two kids growing up in the country. It has listened well.

The sun is warm. It's late afternoon and even later in the summer. Joy and I are lying next to each other on the tender grass watching the clouds skip across the vast, blue soft water pool of sky. There is nothing here that can disturb us. A small herd of cows are grazing in the distance, and the sweet smell of freshly mowed hay lingers in the air to soothe our senses. It's unmistakable; it sure does smell and feel like the home I know. Miller's

Creamery isn't far from here. How often have the two of us gone there together to pick up butter? It has always been a regular sort of thing between us.

Joy's hand feels so soft in mine. She is wearing a yellow flowered sundress with cut lace trim. Her bare arms and legs glisten in the lazy light like satin and remind me that we're both sixteen. We're growing up and the bond between us is only getting stronger... My heart has belonged to this girl all my life. I know that. Nothing is going to change us ever. That is why in four years, I am going to ask her to be my wife.

Shot along like a pair of marbles on a glycerine varnished track, Joy and I are standing at the altar of a country church. I've been here before. It's located in a village called Foxburg, just a few miles north of where we both grew up. She looks so lovely. She's dressed in a beautiful white dress that she's made herself. It took her months of intricate, painstaking embroidery, but she's made it special – just for us... just for today. I look at her with eyes made soft by fondness. There is no amount of love I won't give her. There is no amount of love I can't afford. Her hair done up in rhinestones, her golden curls cascading down about her face, I promise I will cherish her forever, stand by her side and keep her safe. I take her in my arms and kiss her, and she knows that beside me she will always have a place.

We run from the church together, arm in arm and stride in stride... I know without a hint of hardship... without a grain of vice, I'm holding onto the most beautiful bride I could ever imagine... and I have married the most beautiful wife... and with all things good studded in diamonds, we are about to embark on the most beautiful life.

My lovely Joy throws her bouquet of roses and baby's breath away to the wind... to dreams of coming romance... to a young woman's wishes of love. All the happy faces belonging to the small group of well wishers gather outside the church to see us off in our car trailing ebony glass bottles and draft ale cans. We wave goodbye and we're gone like a lightening bolt, further down the tunnel ahead of us. For a place without time, we sure do travel fast.

As though dropped through the roof of a dollhouse, Joy and I find ourselves on the doorstep of our first home together. I playfully sweep her off her feet and carry her across the threshold.

"We're going to spend the next forty years in this house, Honey. We' re going to have lots of babies and fill the space inside these walls with laughter. I'm going to love you so much that you won't know what to do with me half the time and be tickled pink the rest."

"As long as you love me with all of your heart, I won't want for a single thing; I couldn't ask for more," she says with a soft smile and a knowing squeeze of my arm.

I grab her hand and pull her in tight to my body.

"I will always love you with all of my heart."

"I know you will," she pushes through ahead of a kiss, and we're gone again – through the tunnel, into another scene from life. Everything is moving so quickly. It's like we're living our life in snapshots. I remember all the things that have happened in between, but I'm not getting the chance to experience them, though they're still there. I know they happened; I remember them.

Like water down a drain into a cistern, we wash from place to place and year to year – the birth of our daughter Emma... the struggle to make ends meet during the early years. I sell my car so I can afford to buy a stroller, pay the mortgage and buy something special for my wife's birthday. It's a diamond encrusted, gold plated locket. It opens up, and inside I've placed a picture of us when we were kids. It was taken out at the Kennedy farm, a mile down the road from my house. We are sitting on an old broken down swing in front of the barn. No one lived there anymore. All the buildings were falling down. It seemed so empty, yet, somehow, the two of us just being there filled the old place with warmth. That photograph was taken when we were thirteen... Thirteen... Something about that year doesn't seem right... Something happened... Where was Joy? Suddenly I have a sharp pain in my chest. A heaviness has descended upon me from somewhere distant, as though long past and forgotten, yet very much still there. I can tell that Joy is feeling it too, for she is crying.

"What's wrong, my dear?" I ask gently, already feeling the truth.

"I don't know for sure," she answers. "I just feel sad all of a sudden for some reason, but I don't know why."

My beautiful girl looks up at me.

"Forrester, does everything seem alright to you?"

"What do you mean?" I ask, not knowing.

"I mean, does our life seem *normal*? Does it all seem real to you?"

I'm not sure what she's getting at.

"Why wouldn't it? What else can it be but real? It's our life!"

I can tell that she feels sorry she said anything. She knows I'm hurt by it.

"Oh, Forrester, of course it is. I didn't mean it isn't. It just seems like our life is going by so fast... too fast. I'm trying to hold onto it, yet it feels as though it's slipping through my fingers. I can't get a grip on it! I know it's a wonderful life. That's just it, but at the same time, I can't help feeling that something is wrong!"

The most unsettling part is that I know what she means. I didn't quite know how to describe it, but now that she has, it is clear to me that that's what I've been feeling all along; although, caught up in life's moments, it's easy to miss.

"I've noticed it too. It's like I've been mourning over what we've lost – when we haven't even lost it yet. We've got everything. Every moment together is special. I just don't understand why I'm so afraid to see them pass."

Holding onto me tightly, her big blue eyes plead with me not to let go.

"We've got to hang onto every moment. We've got to make them last; I don't want this life to end. I never want to lose you!"

I reassure her the best I can, with all my heart laid open and bleeding truth to all its listeners.

"You will never lose me. I will always be right here by your side where you can see me."

I try to make things light.

"I will stay so close that you'll be sick of me before you know it. You'll be pleading, *When is this going to end?*"

Joy wants to laugh but her worried mind prevents it.

"I never want this to end," her words press firmly into my ears as I feel her arms tighten around my waist.

Nor do I, my lovely girl... Nor do I.

Another flash ahead takes hold of all my senses. Further down the tunnel we slide, and before I know it, we've shot ahead another few years. I'm beginning to see the wear on Joy's face. The persistent push through time has aged her... and me as well. My aches and pains have become too regular, my greying hairs too noticeably there. I wish it were different. It saddens me to see how things change... but more in my wife than myself, for I know it bothers her worse. She's still every bit as beautiful to me.

Again we jump ahead. What we're experiencing is whizzing by at an ever more alarming rate, and the moments are growing lesser by degree. We're at our daughter Emma's college graduation. I look over at Joy, who is seated beside me. I see that she is fighting back tears. I'm holding back a few of my own. Seeing our daughter practically all grown up is close to overwhelming. It seems like only yesterday we brought her home from the hospital and I held her tiny hands. I can remember walking her to the school bus on her first day of school. I can remember the little navy and white dress she wore. I'm recalling camping trips and movie nights and all nature of things in between – first roller coaster rides, trips to the zoo, trips to the dentist and heart to hearts with dear old dad. All of it is there, recoiling back through my memory, every moment we spent as a family – every tear, every smile, every hint of laughter in the air, and there's no denying that our lives were enriched by it all, but now it's behind us – so quickly it's been relegated to the past. It feels as though it has never been anything more than memory, as though it was behind us before we even realized those days were ours to hold... to cherish... to waste. What if we never had them at all – we just think we did? I remember everything as though I lived it. It just doesn't feel lived, that's all. It feels as though I watched it on a screen and read the caption *this was your life* underneath the picture.

Gone again – like a flashbulb exploding before my eyes. we're older still. Joy and I are strolling down a country lane... hand in hand. It's just the two of us again. it's been that way for a while. We're much older now. I can really see it in her face. It's much thinner. She's still pretty, though, in spite of age licking at her edges. Greying hair can't take away her light.

How did we get here? How could we have come so far so fast? Should we not be blessed with much more life ahead of us? Something feels so very wrong.

Resting her head on my shoulder, my lovely wife squeezes my arm.

"We've got to stop this somehow."

At first, I misunderstand.

"Are you getting tired, Honey? Would you like to rest for a bit? We can turn around and head back anytime."

"No, I don't mean our walk. I'm talking about what is happening to us. You've got to feel it too. This isn't natural; our life is racing by way too fast. It doesn't feel real. I can't hold onto anything."

I'm not alone in what I am feeling. I guess there's some comfort in that.

"I feel it too. It feels as though most things in our lives are no more than memories – as though we haven't lived them at all. I remember the events as though they happened, but I can't be sure I was actually there. It feels as though I was for part of them but only for moments at a time. I don't understand why this is happening to us. It's the craziest feeling."

My wife looks at me with fear in her eyes.

"I'm glad it's not only me. I was afraid it was... But why is it happening? Our life has been so fulfilling, yet I'm left feeling so empty, and I'm not sure why."

I shake my head slowly.

"I'm not sure either, though it feels like we've had this conversation before. Haven't we?"

Joy nods her head.

"I think so. It certainly feels as though we have, but I can't say when."

"Neither can I," I agree, "though I know we have. We both know that this isn't right. We're not being given all the time we're owed. I know we're being cheated."

Turning and placing both my hands on my wife's shoulders firmly, I ask her to help us.

"Do you remember anything else?"

I can see my wife struggling for an answer, the frown lines on her brow deepening with every backward thought.

"I remember another life with you... It seems so distant, and it seems as though we were so young. At times, I think it's just a dream... but it seems too real to me, and when I close my eyes, I keep seeing a tunnel. It always feels as though we're walking down a tunnel. The older we get, the harder it is to shake the feeling."

"It's funny you should say that. The memories of us when we were young are the strongest I have – the nearest to feeling real. Everything else, everything that came after is what I wrestle with the most. I just can't be sure about any of it."

Her eyes are so startling and still.

"Oh Forrester, what's happening is scaring me. I am afraid of what is going to happen next."

And just like a shot from a cannon, our world changes again. Another flash of light... another year comes at us from out of the shadows, but it's too far ahead. We shouldn't be here yet. It feels like I was just walking with Joy, but it was years ago... and we weren't this old yet.

Joy is lying in bed beside me. It's our bed... in our house, but she looks so old. Judging by the wrinkled state of my hands, so do I. I'm afraid to look at the rest of me. However, I can see it in my wife's eyes, just as soon as she looks up at me. We're barely recognizable to one another. How many years have passed us by without us knowing... without having a chance to blink an eye?

"What is happening to us?" the old woman beside me murmurs in a hushed, frightened tone.

"I don't know, but I know that much time cannot have passed us by. We were just together and it was at least ten to twenty years ago! I've got more recent memories in my head, but they don't seem real – like we've lived them at all. They are just there in my head taking up space. They're completely hollow!"

My wife nods her head in quiet frustration.

"We can't be this old. It feels as though only yesterday we were still children."

"I know; I feel it too."

All we can do is lie here holding each other to quiet our fear. In my head, I can see the tunnel more and more. As we go down deeper and deeper, it costs us more years. If we slip much further, I fear there will be nothing left. Our lives will be over. It's as though we've been skipping time, and if it happens again... I don't want to think about that; I can't accept it. We've got to stop this runaway train to oblivion! If it really is a tunnel that we've been descending into for the past I don't know how long, then reason would dictate that all we have to do is turn around.

"There is no time... There is no time," a voice floods across my mind, clogging up my senses.

A large white cat stands in the doorway of our room staring down at Joy and I holding each other on our bed.

"If you can find your way back, you'll find your way home."

As soon as the words have purred from his lips, the unusual creature turns and is gone – vanished into the darkness like some sort of ghost. The name Jackson Trigg climbs out of the trenches of my memory into more accessible depths.

"Jackson Trigg!" I scream.

"What's wrong? Who?!" my wife exclaims as she recoils to startled attention.

"Of course! Now I see what's happening."

I grab my wife's hand and pull her off the bed.

"C'mon, Honey! We've got to get out of here!"

She looks confused.

"What?! What do you mean?!"

"Before it's too late, we've got to go back."

"I don't understand – go back where?"

"Back up to the surface – where we came from. We've been going down a tunnel, and if we keep going, it will kill us!"

The more I try to explain it, the more confused she becomes.

"But how? Aren't we in our house?!"

I pull her through the doorway.

"There's no time to explain. We've got to get out of here and fast! If we skip ahead again, we're goners... We might never get back."

Pulling my reluctant wife along behind me, I cut a path through the darkness in the direction I think we came. It's where the white cat seemed to be heading... where he suggested I follow. My heart is thumping inside my chest. It feels as though at any moment, it could happen again and we could get sucked further into the abyss. I know we can't risk another jump ahead; one of us might not be around.

Frantically parting the darkness with my free hand, I forge forth with determined awkwardness. It feels as though we're moving up an incline, which I take to be a promising sign. If it were the opposite, I'd know we were going in the wrong direction.

Back, further up the slope we run. There is less resistance on Joy's end. She seems to be willing and able to move much quicker now. I feel as though I'm getting stronger too. It's too dark to see what we look like, but I feel as though I'm much younger. My energy level is improving and my body is not so sore. I find further assurance in noticing how Joy's hand has become softer. I remember how she used to look... I want to see her that way again.

Things appear to be changing around us. We're not going back through the years – or at least, we're not seeing them manifest before our eyes if we are. I am losing memories, though. I can only recall life with Joy up to a certain point now, and the further back up the tunnel we go, the fewer memories of that time I am able to retain – as though it never happened at all. And in its place, I am finding all manner of things I'd forgotten... My conscious mind sifts through the memory dirt previously buried. A disembodied voice in the darkness offering up words of temptation... offering me a chance at reclaiming something I'd lost... A giant mole named Marik leading me down here to find a little girl... Joy – it was her I'd lost... Pilache the rabbit and the sky full of crows... The humongous white cat called Jackson Trigg, whose purpose is to guide me... Well, at least he showed up when I needed him the most; although, I can't be certain whether he was actually there or not, but I can't be sure of any of it.

It seems like it's working; we're getting away from our fate at the end... at the bottom of this derelict tract. We couldn't have gone much further; it was clear how near we were to vanishing with time. I'm recalling more and more of the events that took place before our fall down the tunnel. Whose voice was it? I couldn't see anything in the darkness. It said I could see the life Joy and I would have had. It never said a thing about not remembering once it was over... though it never said a thing about watching each other die, either. Perhaps if we hadn't turned back, I would have remembered. But what good would it be remembering that? It never said a thing about losing her again. I couldn't bear it! I couldn't risk losing her a second time... To be fair, it did warn of how hard it might be, but I didn't care; I wanted it too badly. I would have given anything to be with her again. By turning around and going back, I might be losing my memory of that golden life we were promised but that's not near as bad as losing the little girl whose hand I have in mine again. I can't let go... As long as I can keep holding onto her, I can't lose her – at least, I want to believe that to be true. Those failing memories are of a life that never happened. It was nice to see, but that much I can do without. In my hand, I feel a real pulse – a real flesh and blood person... one I know I could never do without... one, that now that I have back with me, I will never let go of ever again – not if I can help it... not if I can find a way around things. I don't know how it is possible for her to be here, and I don't know how I'm going to bring her back. I don't even know where we are, really... But if there's a way, I will find it. I will stop at nothing to hold onto her.

Further along, our ascension parades us up to the summit, near the place we began our dive... our fall towards our certain death. The darkness around us is spreading thinner now as more light is finding its way down. For the first time, I can see we're in a tunnel. It's not just some imagined grace. I can make out shapes along the tunnel walls. They are the last escaping recollections of our life undone... what I'd bargained to acquire... what I thought I wanted before I realized the cost – Joy and I lying in the meadow by the forest... the two of us rocking slowly together on the swing... all the things that should have been... all gone now, vanished with the setting sun... but it doesn't set here. It goes on and on as the day is long, for there is no indication of time at all. What a peculiar place I've   fallen   into.

CHAPTER 9

THE CLAW-HAWKS ARE FLYING

As the final shards of memory blister from my mind's illusion, I see the tunnel's end in sight, and in the brilliant light above me, there awaits a giant grey and brown rabbit with a nasty overbite. He towers above the cave's entrance, looking down into the blackness of the hole... searching for someone... waiting for us. His nervous patience is rewarded; Joy and I emerge into the daylight without hesitation. We are glad to be free of all things that bind us below ground. We are desperately in need of air for breathing. Our lungs have been restricted by claustrophobic anxiety for far too long.

"There you are... There you are, my friend," the large furry animal rivets its words in our direction. "I've been sent to collect you and escort you across the swamp."

He looks over at my companion.

"The girl will be safe there."

Seeing Joy standing beside me looking like her old self again, fills my heart with warmth – and a welcome sense of relief. Turning around and hightailing it back out of the tunnel worked like a charm. I think it saved both our lives – certainly Joy's. I have no doubt of that. If we'd continued down that tunnel a little further, we would have died in there. I would have lost Joy for a second time – and most likely for good... and I knew I couldn't bear it. I'm not sure what would have happened to me. I might have survived it – I might have been allowed to walk out of the tunnel as my old self again, but then again, maybe not. Perhaps that is one of the ways the people who wind up here go missing... and the reason why they don't make it back home.

"The whispers in the woods can help you if anyone can."

"Can they help both of us get home?" I ask hopefully.

"Oh, I'm sure they can; they are full of wisdom."

I need to know more about this strange phenomenon, so I continue to dig for information.

"How do you know of them?"

"They speak to us constantly. They advise us in everything we do. They even told me to come here and wait for you."

I'm trying to get my mind around what sort of force we are dealing with.

"Do they know everything that goes on around this place?"

The large furry rodent doesn't even blink.

"They are all knowing. We rely on their direction. They ensure that everything runs smoothly."

"Do you always listen to their advise?" I question, somehow suspecting it not to be optional.

The large creature seems surprised that I would ask such a thing.

"What do you mean?"

"Well, don't you have a choice whether you follow their directions or not?"

"We never question what they tell us to do. We just know to do it. That is how it has always been. It is just how things work around here."

"But how do you know that they are always right? There are many ways to do something. Surely, you can make up your mind for yourself."

I would swear the big rabbit looks frightened.

"Oh, we mustn't do that. We must always listen to the whispers."

"But why?" I demand, thinking this system that they live by to be very unreasonable indeed.

"Because terrible things would happen if we didn't."

"What sorts of things?"

"We would have no protection from the claw-hawks, for one thing. The whispers tell us when it's safe to eat and when it's time to take shelter. Without their direction, we wouldn't stand a chance. Those bloodthirsty birds would pick us off for sure."

"But they almost picked you off today."

"How do you think we knew when to run? The whispers warned us just in time – as they always do."

Come to think of it, I guess that I came the closest to being snatched. All the rabbits were well on their way to finding cover, while I was frozen in place. I reckon that right about then I would have welcomed a voice in my head warning me of the approaching threat.

"Those birds do look dangerous. I guess the voices give you a necessary advantage."

"We couldn't survive in this place without them; there are too many dangers. The swamps are full of carnivorous fish and giant long fanged bush wolves – and if the birds or the fish or the wolves don't get you, the sink holes hidden under the ferns and the grass will swallow you up, or the poisonous thorns on the crab apple trees that grow like weeds around this place will stick you. There are too many ways to lose your life around here – too many ways to reach a conclusion. Without the voice's guidance, none of us would last."

"But I thought there wasn't any time here. Does it really matter when you die?"

I realize the absurdness of my question just as soon as it leaves my mouth.

"Nobody wants to die. We all want to survive. This is all we know, so of course we want to stay here."

"Fair enough. I'm sorry. I'm just trying to figure out how things work in your world."

"Things work very well here. We do as the voice tells us and we live extremely contented lives."

"But does everyone follow the instructions so carefully? Someone mustn't have if you know the alternative."

The rabbit hesitates – nearly choking before speaking.

"Not everyone does. We do have a choice, but very few choose not to heed the advise. The result of ignoring the warnings is always the same – you don't survive."

That does seem harsh.

Are there no exceptions?"

My large furry friend straightens his ears back and shakes his head.

"None. To act against their wishes means certain death."

"So if we choose not to go with you..."

The grey and brown rabbit is still shaking his head.

"You must."

"But why? We're not from your world. How do you know the same rules apply to us?"

The rabbit stares at me solemnly.

"Your kind have come here before. Those who ignore the whispers all meet their end... They don't make it home."

Hmm, not much of a choice at all. Either we obey or we perish. How do you like those apples? What to do... what to do... Considering the dangers that seem to lay in wait around every corner we come to, I don't think it wise to try going it alone. Since the prime objective is to get home and these creatures or forces or whatever they turn out to be are willing to help us do that, the choice appears to be preordained. We continue to do just as we're told. Never mind that earlier advise nearly got us killed – or at least, allowed us to die of natural causes. Following such guidance still throws the best chance at survival our way.

I look over at Joy, still holding onto my hand. Neither of us are willing to let the other go.

We're too afraid that the other would vanish.

"What do you think?" I ask her. "Should we go with him?"

Joy looks frightened and is not sure how to answer.

I ask her again.

"It's up to you as much as me. If we decide to chance it and go it alone, we might get lost or worse. I have to be honest; I have no idea how to get home."

Joy gives me one of her fragile smiles.

"Just promise me you won't leave me. Promise you will never leave me."

She appears so desperately afraid.

I peer deeply into her eyes to reassure her.

"I promise... I will never leave you. I will never let go of you again."

I pull her into my arms and hug her tightly. The warmth between us is felt all the way to my core. I can't deny this feeling. I know she's very real... and I know she's here. She is warm flesh and blood in my hands. There is no way I can be imagining this. Something is troubling me, though. It occupies no more than a small corner in the back of my mind, yet it's still there. It never seems to want to disappear completely. It flashes its warning across the back of my brow like a light on a cliff bidding a ship to be weary. What if my Joy can't follow me home? What if she only exists here in this strange world? What if she's still dead and buried in mine? I don't know if I want to risk taking her back with me. I don't know if I want to chance it. I don't think I could handle the shock of arriving home and finding out that she's not with me... that she couldn't come home after all. To lose her again would just be too much. I don't think my fragile heart could stand it... But she is so real standing here beside me. She's as real as she ever was. I can't help believing she would stay the same wherever we choose to go. We'll arrive home and things will be just as they always were. I will have my Joy again, just like I have her now. I've got to believe it's possible. If not, I should content myself with staying here and trying to survive in this world – whatever this place happens to be. But how can I not want to go back where I belong... to see our farm up on Cabot's Hill... to see my family again. My parents will be worried sick. They won't know what happened to me. Who knows what is going through their heads. They probably think I've been kidnapped. They might draw the conclusion I'm dead.

Suddenly Pilache's large ears stand erect atop his head, as though startled by some danger riding in on the wind.

"What is it?" I have to wonder.

"We must make haste; the claw-hawks are

flying!"

"How do you know? Can you hear them?" I ask, quite sure that the rabbit's large ears could pick up sounds from afar well before any human could possibly hear them.

Pilache shakes his head.

"They are too far away as of yet, even for me. They must fly closer before I can pick up their vibrations. It is the whispers I hear. They are warning me of the claw-hawks' approach."

"But I can't hear a thing."

"That's because you're not tuned into their frequency. You're not of this world, so you're not like us. Your inner ear has not evolved enough to interpret the whispers as anything else but white noise."

"You mean that I will never be able to hear them?"

It's not up to me to say. Such knowledge is beyond me. Only the wise one can answer that kind of question."

It sounds as though *the wise one* is relied upon for an awful lot of things around here, and it hasn't taken long for me to realize that I'm counting on them for quite a bit myself. I certainly hope that they live up to all the hype and can help me half as much as I think they can. Otherwise, I fear I'll remain as lost as ever.

"Will it take long to reach them?" I ask, increasingly eager for a favourable reply.

"No, not long – once we get a move on. I'm not kidding; we must go now. The claw-hawks are flying! They'll be upon us if we don't leave now!"

I look at Joy and she nods in agreement. We both know we can't stay here. We are acutely aware of the constant danger we're in.

"Alright, we're coming. Lead the way and we'll follow."

"Good, good... Let's go then."

Pilache begins to hop off ahead of us.

"We'll stick to the low bush road that skirts along the edge of the swamp. It will offer us much better cover close to the ground. The claw-hawks are less likely to spot us there."

Moving our feet quickly to keep up, we set off after the large furry creature.

"Aren't the swamps too treacherous to risk venturing so near?"

Unwilling to part ways with the energy it would require to turn around, the rabbit enlightens us.

"It's well worth taking our chances; the

birds won't be able to reach us down there. The low lying brambles directly above us will act as a protective shield. If they try to come down on us, they'll become entangled and find themselves trapped and at the mercy of their own kind. They'll turn out to be the catch of the day, not us. If we choose another path, they could descend upon us at will. We would be ripe as crowberries for the picking."

"Yes, but what about the fish in the swamps? Aren't they just as dangerous?"

"As long as we stay out of the water, we'll be quite safe. They can't get to us on land. They're not amphibious."

I guess there's some reassurance to be found in the thought that they can't crawl up onto the road and gnaw away at everything above our boots. I can take solace in that much, at least.

Having to jog along briskly to keep up with the rabbit, Joy and I do our best to blend into the natural woodwork. We've got a ways to go yet before we reach the swamps and the promise of much improved cover. Until then, we are quite aware of our vulnerability. I hold onto the little girl's hand tightly, too afraid to risk letting it go – at least, not until we're out of the woods... or at least, not until we're out of here.

Watching the dark shadows creep ahead of me, I need not look up to tell what lies above us. I'm familiar with the sound of their wings brushing the air in the distance... I know the dead calm before they attack.

"Caw, caw..." I hear them cry.

It's exactly what I've been dreading most. There is still a long ways to go before we reach sufficient cover. Granted, I don't know the lay of the land. I can't honestly say how far away we are from the swamps, but I can tell that there's nothing going to change for at least the next few hundred yards – and those black demons will be upon us by then!

I make the mistake of looking up and seeing a sight worse than anything my mind has yet to conjure. Now my fear truly is complete. From one end of the horizon to the other, the sky is black with birds. Night has descended upon this world for good. Staring into the pitch blackness, my heart is filled with grave doubts whether Joy or I will ever see our home again. Perhaps this is where it all ends for us.

I am very aware that the rabbit is increasing his gate. All I can do is continue to pull Joy along behind me and try to keep up.

"Don't look up; the fear will only slow you down. Keep your eyes on the path ahead. We're almost there. It's just a little further."

I do my best to obey, knowing the sense in his wisdom, but it's hard being so near to intimate danger and not focusing on it above everything else.

At any moment, our lives could end. It's not an easy thing to turn your eyes away from that. There's an overwhelming urge to watch while it happens.

I'm not given a choice; before I can obey, hesitate, act indifferent or run, a large furry paw reaches back and swoops around Joy and I. We are immediately catapulted forward down the path ahead of the creature.

"Don't look back. Stick to the edge of the swamp. Find the wise one in the woods. They will help you find your way," are the rabbit's parting words of encouragement.

As the two of us are sent tumbling head over heels down a steep slope, I hold my eyes open long enough to catch a flash of what we've just left behind. Maybe the speed of the somersaults is messing with my head. I can't say for certain, but I could swear on my mother's undug grave that our friend the rabbit – as big as he already was – has grown another fifty feet in the scant amount of time it has taken me to blink my eyes. How it's possible, I do not know. Though how is anything possible here? None the less, the rabbit now appears to be as tall as the trees.

I complete another rotation down the hill and look up again to see that the rabbit has multiplied by six. Another five giant tree high bunnies have joined Pilache and are meeting the black birds head on in the sky. They have all chosen to stand and fight. I am bewildered that they would do such a thing. Are they doing it just for us? If so, I do feel honoured. Rabbits are usually such timid creatures. It must have taken a lot of courage to risk such a clash.

The killer birds swarm them like diving torpedoes, ripping into their fur with dagger beaks and razor tipped claws. Unwavering, the rabbits swat the winged devils from the sky with their large paws and severe entire heads from the birds' bodies with one chomp of their mighty bucktooth plates.

I tumble round again and turn my eyes once more toward the sky. Like a swarm of black locust hulls, the flock of oversized crows descends upon the noble long eared beasts. Before I lose sight of them again, every last inch of fur has been covered over. Like six black statues, they stagger to and fro, still flailing their paws frantically... still trying to fight off their foes. First, one begins to teeter... then another... and before long – one leading the way for the next, they all go over. They crash to the ground, taking their feathered layer with them, pecking and clawing out chunks of fur all the way down.

Then we're over the slope and too far below to see anymore. All I can hear are the rabbits' horrible screams and the mad, cawing frenzy of the devil birds feasting. The poor things; they sacrificed themselves for us. Why would they do that? Are we really that important? Were they told to do it by the whispers in the woods – or were they driven by their own compassionate hearts? I might never know, though I am grateful for their sacrifice.

Without such a noble effort, Joy and I would have never escaped. We'd be trapped beneath that black robe back there being smothered to death as we speak – and that would have been the best case scenario. We just as easily could have been ripped apart limb by limb before having our heads popped off like the lid of a Coke bottle. It doesn't matter how it would have gone down – a claw through the heart or having our heads snapped off by their beaks; none of it would have been pleasant. All of it we could easily do without, and I am extremely thankful that we have – but extremely sorry that our brave friends weren't so fortunate.

The birds' loathsome, bloodcurdling drone gets drowned out by distance, and I'm thankful for that too. Now our only worries are where we are headed and what further dangers await us. It seems that around every corner awaits some new unwholesome threat. What will it be next time – a serpent, a dragon, some three-headed fish?

Leaving the slope, we tumble into some sort of trench. It more closely resembles a clay trough than anything else. It is smooth and slick and fast, and just as soon as we hit it, we're off like a shot – zipping along the edge of a foul-smelling swamp like a pair of ducks dipped in gravy... like a pair of grain bags tossed down a slippery shoot.

Faster and faster, we slip around corners, between boulders and dive under cover of low lying trees. The rabbit was accurate with his prediction; on this pathway, we're well protected from above –

so well protected that I've lost the sky completely. I just wish we were a little further back from the water's edge. I can hear the water moving when it ought to be still. I'm afraid to look, for I might see something even worse. I've convinced myself it is better to keep my eyes tightly shut and let the momentum either carry me to safety – or at least, some trouble further away.

Down... down... around the curves we slide – the edge of the swamp always within striking distance. All it would take is to reach out too far and an arm or a leg would be in it... And how close would we need to be for whatever is in there to reach us? I sense we're far too near if anything should take the chance to find out. There would be no escape from where we sit. We'd be pulled into the water with one tug, one flip... We'd be pulled under before we knew we were gone. This treacherous road into the heart of the woods might offer protection from the skies but it does nothing to protect us from whatever evil lies at the bottom of the bog. Perhaps there is nothing there; however, it's hard to believe it, for we've already been warned about the giant flesh eating fish that live in its depths, so to hope for an alternative truth would be a very dubious way of thinking, indeed – a path that would certainly set us up for failure. To ignore something doesn't make it go away, and it makes you no less vulnerable if you choose not to take the necessary precautions. It simply makes you a fool – and this world tends not to prosper a fool terribly well. From what I've seen so far, it chews them up and spits them out faster than rain ricocheting off the hard, shiny surface of a taut metal roof.

However, as aware of the potential trouble at hand as I am, I can't do much about it other than continue my slide, hopefully bypassing most of it in the process. We seem to be going extremely fast and that should help us – at least, that's what I've been telling myself. I'm trying to convince myself that keeping ahead of danger is the nearest thing we've got to playing it safe.

Down... down we slide... We appear to be spiralling ever deeper into the bog. The woods where we started out are so far above us now that I'm sure they've blended into the sky... if it weren't tarred black with crows... if I could still see it from where I sit now under the dense branches of the low lying trees. How we'll ever reach the heart of the woods from here, I do not know... unless we were never intended to. Perhaps the rabbit meant to send us to the bottom of the bog... Maybe he wanted us to die. But why would the lot of them give their lives for that? It makes no sense – but neither does this. How can the trajectory we're on possibly be leading us deeper into the woods – when it's only taking us down?

"Ah!"

Oddly, Joy's scream is the first thing that alerts me to a decline in our fortunes, though it should have been the water seeping into the seat of my pants. We've reached the end of the road! I can't prevent myself from going into the water and neither can Joy. She's practically on top of me. We're doing this together. Sink or swim, we'll either survive this mess or die trying. We haven't got a choice.

CHAPTER 10

BENEATH THE MURKY DEPTHS

"Sploosh!"

We're up to our necks in foul smelling water.

"Help, Forrester! Help me! Don't let me drown!" Joy screams in between frantic breaths.

"I've got you!" I assure her, doing my best to keep her head above water. "Don't worry; I'll get us out of here!"

I can feel the bottom with my feet, though I feel them sinking. I'll need to half swim, half claw my way out of this soup – and that is exactly how I endeavour to keep us afloat.

"There's something down there! I can see it moving closer!" Joy warns in sheer terror.

I want to deny it, but I can see it too. I'm trying like crazy, but I just can't move fast enough. The edge of the swamp is still too far above us. We can't get away from whatever is after us!

I see a row of razor sharp fins breaking the surface of the water. I'm sure I see teeth and blood-speckled eyes. Whatever this creature is, it smells horrible... like the foulest sewer imaginable... like its belly is full of rot. It causes me to wonder who its last victim was and how long they've lay in its stomach.

The large fish rises above the water – well, half out, half in. Much of its mass yet lies submerged, but the water close to the surface is strangely clear. I can see its sleek body. I am in shock at what my eyes entreat me. It's quite a beautiful creature. It shimmers silver and gold... with a bluish tint to it. It's not ugly at all. It's quite captivating, actually. It is joined on the surface by another – and then another. Before long, there are half a dozen encircling the two of us. I know I ought to be more frightened than I am, but I can't help being mesmerized. With their fins gently fluttering from side to side and their soft gills pushing out the water, they leave you with a very calm impression – and that might be where the greatest danger lies. They have the ability to virtually lull their victims to sleep.

I find myself unable to move. It doesn't matter how much part of me wants to get Joy and myself out of this pool and closer to safety; my muscles are not responding. Everything capable of making a move is apparently sleeping. Perhaps that is how all their prey succumb to their charms. If it weren't for the unmistakable smell of death hanging about them, I would be fooled completely. Although, even with it, it hardly seems enough of a deterrent, for when I ought to be running, I find myself to be entirely frozen in place. It's not till the giant tuna fish open their mouths to reveal their ugly insides do I feel a straining on my limbs. The rows of jagged, razor sharp teeth grinning in our direction now distracts away from everything else. Fear has arrived with all its fever pitted resistance from wherever it has been hiding up until this point. The trouble is that now it's too late to run. As soon as we turn our backs, these creatures are sure to be on us. They'd rip us to shreds before we set one foot on the shore. We might not have had much of a chance before, but now I'm certain we've got nothing even remotely resembling hope. I might be able to get Joy out in time. I think that is the best I can hope for. If I keep myself between them and her, I will take the brunt of the attack while she scrambles to safety. I don't know what will become of her without me, but I've got to try to save her, none the less. It's why I came here in the first place... It's why I'm here at all. And if I can't save her, at least then we might be together. Maybe that's the real reason I've come here. Perhaps this is how it was always to end.

I turn and look into Joy's eyes. I realize that I know nothing for certain, but she's just as alive and real as anyone can be right at this moment. I don't see how she could be any more so... She's flesh and blood in my hands, and all I know is that I'm finding it incredibly hard telling her she has to go.

"You've got to go now! Push off of me toward those rocks. Just get yourself out of the water and don't look back. I'll keep those things busy. It's your only chance."

By the look in her eyes, I know she understands what I'm telling her to do, but she's not liking it one bit.

"But what about you? They will kill you!"

I shake my head.

"Don't worry about me. There is no other choice. we've got to get you to safety. I'll take my chances."

I try to leave some shred of hope intact.

"With a bit of luck, we might both get out of this alive."

My efforts are greeted with a whole lot of hesitation. I'm not sure whether she's going to heed my advice and head for the rocks or not. She's just staring at me, as though saying, *How can you ask me to make such a choice? How can I possibly leave you?* I know it's unfortunate to find ourselves in such a situation where I have to ask, but since we do – and since I do have to ask, it must be clear that there is no choice. She's got to go now! I can tell by their twitching that the fish are getting ready to attack.

Just when we need a saviour the most, we find one. From out of nowhere, the seas are parted and in walks a set of familiar whiskers. The big white cat, Jackson Trigg, appears behind us. He wastes no time at all in springing into action. One claw-tipped paw darts out like a springbok racing across the desert and grabs hold of its prize. The nearest fish is plucked from the water and tossed upside down on the shore. The large silver minnow doesn't look nearly so threatening flopping around on its back gasping for air.

The rest of the fish immediately scatter, disappearing beneath the murky depths. I'll take a close call narrowly avoided over being eaten alive, anytime. I truly thought I was a goner. We have reason to rejoice; hope for Joy and I remains alive and breathing.

"I clearly can't leave you alone for long without you getting yourself into trouble," the cat relates. "I warned you about the dangers lurking around this place. I should have known you wouldn't take me seriously. Now look at what nearly happened. You were almost fish bait."

I know we owe him a lot of thanks for coming to our rescue, but I hate having him think we've been entirely helpless on our own.

"We couldn't help it; we fell down the slope and couldn't stop. We tumbled right into the water. We'd heard about the fish that live here, and believe me; it's the last place we wanted to wind up."

The cat looks confused.

"Why were you so careless?"

"We weren't. We were trying to get away from the crows and Pilache the rabbit threw us ahead of him. That's how we wound up falling down the hill."

Jackson shakes his head.

"Trading one danger for another is never a sound proposition. And who is the *we* you keep referring to?"

I'm the one who looks confused now.

"What do you mean?"

"Who was with you during all this?"

"Why, my friend Joy, of course."

Suddenly aware I'm no longer holding onto her hand, I turn to face her... only to realize she's no longer there. I immediately panic.

"Joy! Joy!" I'm frantic. "Where did she go?!"

Oddly, the cat remains completely calm.

"There is no one here but you."

I don't know what he's talking about.

"What?! But you must have seen her. She was right here beside me. She hasn't left my side since I found her down in the tunnel. I want to take her back home with me. That's why we're trying to find the voice in the woods. Pilache said it can help us."

Jackson's calmness deteriorates little when faced with my words of protest.

"It has always been only you."

I'm not buying it for one minute.

"You don't know what you're talking about. She was just here. She's been here all along."

I'm really starting to panic now. What happened to her? Did she go under?! Did one of those huge nasty fish drag her down?!

"Joy... Joy!" I scream. "She must have gone under! I've got to find her!"

There's no time to waste. I dive under the water and frantically begin to search around in the murky wasteland. It's difficult to see more than a few inches in front of me, for there is as much mud as there is water. The water can't be more than six feet deep, nor is the pool we're in very substantial, though it's plenty large enough for a little girl to get lost in.

In spite of my blindness, I comb the shallow trench for as far as it reaches. Swatting through the water at imaginary spectres and feeling as deeply into the mud and weeds as I can for anything resembling substance. I've lost all fear of the fish's presence – and not just because I believe they've all fled and disappeared through one of the narrow troughs into another pool further inland. All I'm concerned about is my lovely girl, Joy. I can't let her drown! I can't lose her again! If even a small part of me doubted it before, now I know it for certain. She means everything to me. There is nothing more precious. I know I would give my own life to save hers. It isn't a question. It is nothing short of my greatest desire. I'm content to do it if it's required of me... if I have to. I wouldn't think twice. It's become entirely automatic – a mandatory requirement of my heart, for it can't go on beating without her... It can't pump blood through my veins if she no longer stands beside me... though it's my most coveted wish to spend my life with her... as I saw it down in that dark tunnel... as I lived it when I wasn't really there.

I have no choice but to come up for air.

"Gasp!" I break through the surface of the algae and draw air into my aching lungs. Before I even open my eyes, I'm made aware that Jackson Trigg is still there.

"You cannot find what is not there," he insists. "She was never there, Forrester, and she's not here now. You've only seen what you wanted to see. You're wasting your energy; you won't find a thing but mud and cat tail roots down there."

I don't know why he's giving me such a hard time. I know I haven't been imagining it. Joy is as real as anything here... She's as real as me... In my mind and heart, she's as real as real can be. She was here! I know it. I looked into her eyes, I held onto her hand... and I held her... I spoke with her... I know she was here with me; I felt her beating pulse pressed into mine. I've got to find her. I have to ignore him and find my beautiful girl. It is not a matter that's up for debate. There is no other acceptable option.

I suck two lungfuls of air back in through my mouth and nostrils and once again return under water. I do this repeatedly until there is nothing more to search – not in the water, not in the mud on the bottom of the lagoon, not in the reeds creeping up the edges onto the shore... I've contented myself that she's not there, yet I can't be content at all; she's got to be somewhere. She couldn't have disappeared completely, for I know she was here a minute ago.

Exhausted, I drag myself back up to the surface and relate, "It's impossible! I can't find her! I don't understand it. Where did she go?!"

"You cannot find what isn't there," is all that finds its way back to my troubled ears. It rains down upon them like the worst sort of pretense of the very thing I've been dreading to hear. And the worst of it is, the more I hear it, the more I'm beginning to believe it has merit – and that is the thing that scares me the most.

"But she was here... I'm sure of it," I continue to insist.

It is time for a change in the direction of the conversation.

"You must be very cold," Jackson Trigg commiserates.

Suddenly, I'm aware of the water's frigid temperature. What's more of it, I realize I'm thoroughly chilled to the bone. In fact, my body is so numb that I can barely feel it. I know if I don't get out of this ice water bath immediately, I will surely fall into hypothermic shock. If that happens, I'll slip under and not be able to resurface by my own accord. I am so thoroughly exhausted that I can barely keep my head above water. I am physically and emotionally drained. I don't know what to think. Where could Joy have gone? She was just with me... If I hadn't let go of her hand, I wouldn't have lost her again... I don't even remember letting it go.

Jackson sees my struggle and decides to intervene. He bends down and grabs hold of me by my shirt collar with his strong jaws. When I saw his mouth open and the rows of sharp teeth moving towards me, I thought he was going to take my head off, so I'm incredibly relieved that he bypassed my flesh completely. One swift motion plucks me out of the water and sets me onto dry ground. I am thankful for the assistance. If I'd been left in the pot under my own devices, I fear I would have gone under at any moment and not resurfaced. I had just about given up on everything.

I lie here on the flat rock and work hard at catching my breath. I am feeling the cold from being soaked to the bone and find myself unable to stop shivering. I very nearly died in that cesspool. First I was one hair away from being eaten by giant, foul-breathed fish, then I almost drowned from exhaustion, and now I find that it doesn't matter so much to me that I'm alive at all. What's the point without Joy, anyhow? I'm entirely lost and alone in this strange world – with only these giant fur-bearing animals for company, and they're not much company to cling to. They speak in cryptic tongues and seem content on losing me. Ever since my arrival, at best I feel they've sent me on a wild goose chase, and at worst I think they're trying to kill me. I have yet to make up my mind whether I should look upon them as my friends or the enemy. This large cat did just save my life. I must admit to that obvious truth, so maybe I'm wrong about them having more sinister intentions... and the rabbits did appear to sacrifice their lives so that Joy and I would survive – though they nearly delivered us to our deaths by a different route. My mind is still not made up about what the mole's true intentions encompassed. He seemed genuine enough; he helped me find Joy. It wasn't his fault we nearly came to an end down in the tunnel. It was the mysterious disembodied voice that I struck the bargain with. I'm sure the mole was no more than a pawn – like the rest of the animals here. They are helpless – controlled by the whispers that work their way into their thoughts.

The large fish lying beside me gasps very irregularly now. They are infrequent exertions. Its entire body convulses each time it makes such effort. The slippery creature is no more than a few feet from where I've been left clinging to the ground – and its teeth are even closer, but it seems far from threatening now. In its dying throes, it has no desire for anything beyond reaching for one more breath. In spite of its size... and its potential to slice me open with one swipe of its razor like teeth, or squash me with a single wayward flop in my direction, I see no real cause for fear. It can barely move now and looks nothing more than something pathetic and sad. How quickly a noble creature diminishes once you take away its strength... once you strip it of the thing it needs the most.

Its silver gills sparkle in the sunlight streaming through the gaps in the foliage above me. I turn my eyes once more towards the sky. I wonder if it is the same sky I've seen every single day of my life... I wonder how close I am to home... Am I willing to go back there without Joy... without the true sunshine in my life?

I contemplate where I've landed. The trees above me reach hundreds of feet into the air. They stretch out their long branches like fingers on mighty hands. They try to cover the blue of the heavens from showing its worth. Enough light makes it through to see everything clearly – or so I am led to believe. Perhaps much lies hidden in the shadows that keep us company here. Perhaps there is much that goes unseen. That could be why I am having such difficulty finding my way home.

Looking around me, I see flowers that appear darker than they should. Their colours are vibrant. Rich reds, velvety blues and deep purples wash their petals over the ground. They fall like enormous snowflakes onto the lush carpet of grass beneath them. They litter the landscape with fragrant ruin.

The immense white feline looms above me.

"What do you want now?" the overgrown kitten purrs.

Gradually regaining my strength, I respond the best I am able.

"I want to find my friend Joy, and I want to take her back home."

The cat rolls his large eyes and throws his head back in exasperation.

"Your friend is not here!" he allows his voice to fall down upon me heavily.

"But I know she is. I found her in the tunnels and she's been with me ever since. I know she has; I was holding onto her hand."

Jackson looks smug, his fat feline face curling up into something resembling a scowl.

"Then, where is she now?" he insists.

I look around me and see no sign of what invades my heart with the most intensity.

"I don't know. I've lost her again, it seems. I

let go of her just for an instant and she disappeared."

"She wasn't here at all. She's only alive in your head – and be thankful for it, for if you did find her here, you could never go home."

"Why not?" I demand.

"She's not there anymore. She doesn't exist in either of our worlds. She is gone and you must accept that."

I find myself pleading with the big cat desperately.

"But I can't accept it! I can't live without her. She means everything to me. I must find her again and bring her back with me."

Jackson Trigg slows his voice and eases into his words again.

"If you want to see your home again, you must let her go."

"But I can't; I am lost without her!" I plead, with every last shred of hope clinging to my words of appeal.

"If you don't, then, I can't help you. You'll just be lost."

"But what does that mean? Will Joy be with me if I stay here?"

I sense a hint of compassion in the cat's voice.

"She's not *really* with you now. She's only a figment of your imagination. She's not really here, Forrester. You must understand that. If you stay here, you will go on searching endlessly for something that doesn't exist – and because of it, you'll never find your way home."

"What will happen to me then?"

"You will drift from place to place until you reach some unkind end. As I've told you before, this is a dangerous place. Without my help, you are liable to perish."

I'm finding it all very hard to accept.

"But she feels very real to me here. Back home, I never felt her that way – not after..."

"Not after she *died*, Forrester. You need to say it. You have to accept it. She's not there anymore. She's dead and buried. She rests beneath the ground now. She no longer walks upon it."

"No-o-o!" I scream. "I can't accept that! I need her to be here with me!"

Jackson Trigg hangs his head in disappointment.

"Then, I am sorry, but I can't help you. The choice is yours to make, but know that you will never see your mother or father again. You will not see your home. I have to ask you – can you live with that?"

I have to think about it for a moment. Would I be able to accept never seeing my home or family again? Would it be worth giving up to be able to spend my days with Joy – even if it's only in my head... even if it's just for so long a duration? Would spending one more day with her be worth it?

I'm a little surprised by the briefness of my deliberation, though not really; I know the truth in my heart.

"I would give anything to be with Joy again. I would trade my parents' lives... I would trade my own. I would trade every last memory of home if I believed there was a chance I could spend more of my days beside her."

"Then, there is no helping you, I'm afraid, for there is nothing here that you seek. Your friend doesn't exist here, and there is no time to be had. There is only the here and now – one long, drawn out, continuous moment until you are gone... vanished from this world as well as your own, for if you are lost here, you will certainly be lost to your own. It's a lot to give up for something that's not really there... for something already lost."

In spite of the logic behind his argument, there's no convincing me, for I know what she's worth.

"She's worth every effort; she was the

greatest friend in the world."

Jackson Trigg shrugs his shoulders and begins to walk away.

"Then, you've made your choice. I wish you luck."

I'm suddenly very aware of my reluctance to let him go.

"But what if I need help? Will you still be there?"

Turning, the white cat fixes his gaze upon me with narrowing eyes that seem content on pinching out every last flicker of light.

"Consider yourself to be on your own. You can't count on me coming to your rescue; I might not know you're in danger. You see, by making the choice that you have, you've severed our connection. I'm not responsible for you anymore. Your fate rests entirely in your own hands now."

With nothing more to say, the big cat vanishes into the undergrowth of the forest, which now appears very clearly to spread out from the edges of the swamp – in every direction but one, for a steep slope climbs up the hill Joy and I slid down.

With Jackson gone, I'm feeling very much alone. The stagnant pools of water lie still and sour beneath my nostrils, and the trees that stretch out ahead of me conceal any sign of life. I don't know how I am going to find my Joy again. Now I'm not even certain if she's ever been here at all. Maybe what Jackson said is the truth; she is nothing more than a figment of my imagination... a hollowed out memory that keeps haunting my mind. Am I really willing to give up everything for a story in my head... for thoughts of what might have been – if Joy were actually still around... not dead and buried... not lying six feet under the cold hard ground? If it weren't for her appearing so real to me in this world... giving me hope that she could still be alive... If it weren't for that sparkling stone blinding my eyes, I very well might give in to reason and be content to go home alone. However, she does come alive for me here. She gives me what I followed her down to this underworld to find – a chance to be with her again... more moments in her company... the thing I've been seeking all along – more time. Even though Jackson claims it doesn't exist, what else could it be? Even if it is just one long drawn out moment, it seems to last. It's as good as time, if you ask me – maybe better. Things can't get old that way, and neither can we.

All I have to do is find my Joy again. As long as I can do that, I will be content to stay here. I would like to be able to go home, though only if I can take her with me. If I can't – if that's not possible, then I am quite willing to take my chances in this world.

What did my friend Pilache tell me? *Go find the source of the whispers in the woods. If anyone can help you, they can.* I might not be able to hear them myself, but if I can somehow find them, surely they will help me. If I can't find Joy on my own, they can show me where she is... and perhaps they can help the two of us get home. Pilache seemed to think they had the power to achieve such wonders. He seemed able to see Joy too. I don't know why Jackson Trigg is so blind to her presence. It is as though he is unwilling to believe she is there... to believe in the possibility that she could exist. I don't understand it; he seems to want to help me – and he certainly saved my life. I don't know why he is unwilling to assist me with what I truly desire – the thing that means the most in the world to me. Perhaps he knows something that Pilache didn't. I hope not; the possibilities that the rabbit presented are far more appealing. They are much more in line with what I want to hear.

CHAPTER 11

MYSTERIOUS FIGURES IN THE SHADOWS

I set out upon the pathway that hugs the swampland. It etches a border around the edge of the bog as fine as a ribbon separating strands of hair. There's barely a space between the water and the ground I set foot upon. If I make one errant step, I could wind up back in that slimy syrup. I'm sure that those nasty fish have already worked their way back. With Jackson gone, there is no longer anything keeping them at bay. They might get brave and jump up out of the water to try to pull me in, and chances are I won't have the fat cat coming to my rescue next time.

I feel far from safe walking this pathway I've chosen to tread. The sooner I leave the swampland behind the better. As I peer over my shoulder into the marsh, I can already see the dark water churning as though a hundred of those vicious creatures are brooding just below the surface.

I start to run. I've got to get away from here before the tension worsens... before those foul things get to me... before I'm pulled back in. I'm nearing the far end of the swamp. Just another couple hundred yards and I'll be clear. Though I'm running as fast as I can, I know they're getting closer. I can hear their tails striking the water with deliberate intent. The sooner they run out of water the better; it is the only way to prevent a horribly unpleasant reunion – one I'll do my best to avoid.

Just a little further. I'm almost there. Oh God, let me make it; I don't want to be eaten alive! I can hear them behind me. They're practically on my heels now. I can smell their vulgar breath. The edge of the forest is within a few desperate strides. I lunge forward like I haven't a prayer if I do anything else. I hit the ground and roll several times into the long grass. I've made it! I'm clear of the bog and its unholy keepers. I look back in time to catch the killer fish leaping and snapping at the water's edge. I can see the flash of their razor sharp teeth and the throbbing veins in their bloodshot eyes. They are shaking and twisting in anger over the loss of their intended meal. I'm very aware that I've gained the forest just in time. If I'd been on that path any longer, I'm certain they would have gotten to me. They would have grabbed me by my ankles and pulled me in. It would have been the cruellest of ends, though perhaps that is the only way I'll ever truly see Joy again. Perhaps I need to be dead for that to happen. Although, if it does have to be that way, I would wish for a gentler end – one using less teeth and tearing of flesh.

As the upset in the waters behind me quiets, I raise myself off the ground and take my first steps into the forest. I hesitate just briefly; I wonder what danger awaits me next. Jackson Trigg is right about that much. This world is not a safe place to be lost in. If others have come here, as he claims, it is no wonder they perished. There are far too many pitfalls to make it out of here without some kind of help. Jackson was meant to help me. Perhaps I was a fool to refuse him, but what else could I do? I've come here to find Joy, and I'm not leaving without her. I can't... I refuse to surrender my hope – and that is the reason I continue here on my own. I am hoping that someone can help me. I hope to find my Joy again – and yes, I still hope to get home. The mole and the rabbits were trying to help me – at least, I think that was their honourable intention. I'm counting on the mysterious voice being just as generous. If it can't – or is unwilling to help me, I'm not sure where I'll turn. I'm short on options and I'm very aware of that. I know I'm operating solely on faith now.

Deep into the forest I wander. The giant trees rise above me to crowd out the sky. Their branches coil overhead to form a near penetrable dome, and the further I go into the forest, the less light is allowed in. It's dark in here. It's hard not to feel intimidated by the silence... and the denseness of shadow. The scant rays of light trickle down through the canopy like fluttering leaves, falling lazily about me every few feet. They are quite pretty to look at and provide just enough illumination to guide me. It is quite a surreal place to find myself lost, though I can't say for certain that I'm not exactly where I'm supposed to be. I don't know where I'm going. I can't deny that; however, I do believe I'm travelling in the right general direction. I just don't know how long it will take to get there, that's all, and I can't even be sure I'll find what I'm looking for. I'm only going by what Pilache told me. I'm trusting that what he said is the truth – that there is something deep in the forest that can help me. For all I really know, I could be walking into some sort of trap. Perhaps the rabbits weren't trying to help me at all. But then why would they protect us from the crows, and furthermore, sacrifice their own lives over it? They must have thought our lives to be important. Their actions wouldn't make sense any other way.

I'm not sure how I'm going to find whatever is behind a voice that I can't even hear. I'm not sure exactly what I'm supposed to be looking for. The voice I heard down in the tunnel before I found Joy didn't appear to have any kind of physical form. I don't know if this is the same thing or if it's something entirely different. I don't know what exactly I'm supposed to be looking for. At this point I don't have much choice, though it's the only chance I think I've got. It's the only lead I have to go on. If this mysterious ghost in the forest can't help me, I'm not sure what I'll do.

Further I tread blindly, unknowing of my true destination. The dark woods are a strange place, much more uncertain than the forest on higher ground. With more trees and less light, it's the perfect place to get lost. I am frightened and wishing that I could find my way back into the light.

As though my wish has been heard and granted, a slight tear in the ceiling of leaves above me opens up to allow a ray of sunlight to fall before me like a path. It makes perfect sense to follow it, so I do exactly that. It sure beats continuing to stumble blindly through the dark. Regardless, I'm choosing to believe that it has been put there to guide me – like a torch lit up to show the way.

Buoyed by my new sense of direction, I quicken my step moving forward, and for some reason, I don't feel quite as scared. I only wish I didn't feel so utterly alone. Without Joy beside me, I truly am miserable. I wonder what the point of me coming here was if not to be with her. I could have fared just as well back home. Why come here at all if I wasn't meant to save her? I'm feeling more empty than ever now. Finding her only to lose her again is too crushing a blow to swallow. I'm not quite certain what I believe at the moment, but it seems I was given a peek at a lifetime with her – and that wasn't even enough to content me. It didn't seem truthful enough... I will tell myself that, but mainly, I don't think it lasted for nearly long enough. That was the real evil in its merit. I yearned for the real thing. Just as long as she was near me, my heart could be contented. However, now that she's left me again, I feel the loss more than ever before. Surely, someone or something here can help me. I pray I'm getting close to such a chance.

There is just enough light falling down through the leaves to paint the shadows darker still. They haunt the illusion of something better only to let you down as soon as you cast an eye closer to their true intent. A more detailed viewing shows they hide something ugly. The trees in this place are gnarled and twisted with bumps and abrasions weighing them down. They scream of pain and discontent in every impression upon their weary trunks. What sights must they have seen to have to live with such an unfavourable indent. Their roots must have soaked up a lot of suffering to grow such pitiful fruit.

It's hard to feel good after noticing the changing landscape around me. Other than the slim trail of light leading me onward, the woods appear to be getting darker the further I fall into their midst. I am growing more uneasy with every faltering step I push forward. There is something about this place that seems worse than the rest. I feel a sickness very much present that was not there before.

There is no time for any serious lament. As sudden as I thought it, things have taken a turn for the worse. A strong wind whips its way between the trees, wrapping its swirling arms around me in a most unwelcome embrace. Leaves are shattered from the branches above me and hurled down upon my head like paper thin raindrops filled with lead. There are too many to get away from, so I pull my jacket up over my head and defend against the onslaught the best I can. I try to run but am driven to a standstill by the wind coming at me from all directions. I can be blown forward just as easily as back, so there is no sense in changing direction. Even standing still isn't a very good bet; I could be crushed by a massive tree branch just as likely glued to one spot. I keep struggling forward until I reach a rock overhang. I crawl under it, deciding it's my best bet at a time like this.

Just when it seems the storm could go on forever, the churning air dries up and all returns to normal. Once the last leaf has settled for a home, the only lingering sign of recent trouble are the gaps of sky above me. I'm guessing nearly being torn apart by the gale force winds was worth the effort; the lack of a solid ceiling overhead lets more light in. Perhaps now I'll be able to see where I am to go.

Branches litter the ground, so I have to be careful not to trip. It is still dark enough in these woods to get lost in the shadows cast by crooked trees and gnarled wood, bramble bush and thicket. If I stare into the darkness for long enough, I start to see unusual figures resembling men. They dance in the shadows like smoke swirls rising up from a fire. Except in this case, everything is turned upside down, with the sky above me acting as the flames and the mysterious figures in the shadows, their children. I'd be best not to stare into their midst for too long; I might see something I don't want to see.

The hairs rise up on the back of my neck like a row of soldiers getting set to shoot their next volley. I fear I've allowed my eyes to linger too long. I swear the figures are already in full motion... and more are coming out from behind the trees. I'd better close my eyes and forget these horrid thoughts without delay, for whatever foul instruments have formed in my subconscious mind have taken shape and are moving towards me.

As the figures pass into the light stream cast down from above, I can see what they really are. Ironically, I recognize them as familiar. They are like me... They are children.

"Who are you?" the first one to step forth questions in a soft but hollow tone.

I'm not sure if I should answer; I find it hard to believe this is real. It is the last thing I thought I'd find in these woods.

"You're not one of us," the fair haired boy cautions without any response. "You are new here."

The persistence of his words forcing their way deeper into my rational mind, I can't help but answer.

"No and yes, I am new here – fairly new, at least. I just got here, I think. Since my arrival, I've lost track of time."

All the children laugh in unison.

"Ha! You ought to know better; you won't find anything like that here," they giggle.

"So I've been told, though I don't quite understand it. I don't see how it's possible for time not to exist."

The boy smiles without changing the expression upon his lips.

"There is no need of it in a place like this. Nothing ever changes. You're either here or you're not. No one ages. We will never grow old."

"But things do change. I've seen it firsthand. I've seen animals killed by vicious birds. Their lives surely changed. One moment they were alive, the next they were dead!"

The boy bothers to change his expression little.

"You're either here or you're not," he reiterates, as though it is vitally important to know this. "The things you've witnessed matter little. Everything exists just the same. The sun shines above the treeline, the leaves blow in the wind, the animals feed... Days don't change, nor do they turn into night. No plant is bigger than it was last you saw it, no moment colder than the next. Everything moves along on one long constant continuum – always the same, all of it securely held in place."

After witnessing life here firsthand, I'm finding it hard to believe.

"But it's just an illusion. I've seen the weather change. A storm blew in just moments ago. There are branches on the ground that weren't there before. Of course things change. They're changing all the time. Anyone can die here. Things can change forever!"

An olive skinned girl steps forth to respond to my protest.

"The wind will blow just the same next time you walk through this part of the forest and the exact same branches will fall. You're either here or you're not. Those things have no bearing on time whatsoever. No one remembers you being here, for there is no past to remember."

It's an intriguing concept, though sadly, one that's not that different from my own reality. I wonder how long it will take for me to forget all about Joy. I don't want to believe that I will ever be able to, and I don't think I will, but who knows, people do such things all the time.

"Aren't you afraid of dying?" I ask them, well aware of the dangers that are ever present, just waiting, half hidden behind every bend.

"Black Bobbin keeps us safe. We only know peace now."

"Who?!" I ask, taken aback, startled by the name's introduction.

The children are all gathered around me now, making me feel increasingly claustrophobic. There must be at least fifteen of them. I'm finding it quite unsettling how they've gathered around me and have begun to hum a haunting refrain.

"Black Bobbin, Black Bobbin... He's coming to get you. He will find you in the meadow. He will find you in the forest. He will take you in," they sing together. "Black Bobbin, Black Bobbin... You can't resist him. He knows what lies inside your heart. You will follow him down the pathway. He will lead you through the dark."

The children's song is at once soothing and disturbing. I'm feeling uneasy upon hearing it. I'm afraid to meet the inspiration for their verse.

"This *Black Bobbin* you sing about... Is he a man or some sort of animal?" I beg of them, worried that he's both.

Their hurried and chased response does little to lessen my anxiety.

"He *is* both. He's a man and he is an animal. He is everything and like nothing else. He is the whispering wind and the echo on the horizon. He is that voice inside your head and the ache in your guts that tells you not to do something. He is your conscience and your guilt. Once you let him in, you'll find it's impossible to do without him. You'll depend on him for everything from then on in."

I'm not liking the sound of this at all.

"Is he the voice that the animals hear – the one that instructs them on what to do?"

"Everyone here depends on him for guidance. Most only know him as a voice, but without his assistance, everyone would be lost."

"But does he really help you? It sounds like he controls you more than anything," I offer as an honest response.

The girl standing directly in front of me seems surprised I would even suggest it.

"Nothing would exist here without him. Without his generosity, we would have been lost."

Another question arises in my mind that I've been aching to ask.

"Where do you come from? Are you from my world? Did you get lost down here too?"

They are all questions to which I'm sure I already know the answer. They are children just like me, and Jackson Trigg, the white cat, said there have been others.

"We were all just like you. We each had a home in your world like you did. We found this place because we were searching for something. After wandering on our own to no ends, we realized that Black Bobbin was the only one who could help us, and he can help you too."

"I hope he can," I answer. "That is why I've come here. I don't know where else to turn."

"What is it that you desire?" a booming voice threatens from behind the trees.

In response, the children scatter in all directions. They seem awfully timid in the presence of someone who is supposed to mean so much to their well being.

"It's Black Bobbin... It's Black Bobbin,"

they whisper, their timid voices half buried beneath
their   obvious   fear.

CHAPTER 12

BLACK BOBBIN

I look up to see a creature towering nearly as high as the trees. My eyes lead me on a journey up its shaggy hair covered legs rising above a pair of hooves. It has the torso, arms and head of a man – except for the set of mighty, curving horns with serrated edges that look as though they could gut a sow. A tuft of course black hair decorates its chin and compliments the mane crowning its bony brow and running down the entire length of its back. Its skin is dark and leathery and appears oily and course with prickly hairs bristling out in all directions. A strong odour pervades the air from dank origins, making me want to hold my breath and turn away. What have I gotten myself into? A more threatening creature I could not find in my worst nightmares. Even the pterodactyl-like crows and killer fish pale in threat and vice next to it. Now I truly believe the rabbit was trying to get me killed when he sent me down this path. I should have listened to Jackson. He seems to be the only one here dispensing sound advice. Perhaps he's been the only one on my side all along, though how was I to know any of it? He wasn't telling me what I wanted to hear. That is why I refused to listen. Perhaps I wanted more than I had the right to ask and that is why I've wound up here in the company of the devil. With his horns and hooves and broken, hooked teeth, he is the complete embodiment of the myth. I couldn't imagine a more loathsome overlord of the abyss. It's no wonder the children act so frightened. Even when they were praising all his merits, I could hear the hesitation in their voices. They are scared. I wonder what they got in return for their allegiance. I wonder if it was worth giving up their souls to find out. I wonder if it will be worth it for me.

As the huge horned devil stares down at me with fire dipped eyes, I know he's waiting for an answer. At this point, I know it is impossible to run. All he'd have to do is reach down with one large hand to snatch me up into my ruin. No, I have no choice but to face him. If I reason with him, perhaps he'll let me live. After all, I did come here for a reason, and I'm not going to leave without first begging him for his help. I've got to see this through; I won't be able to live with myself if I don't. If there is a chance at all that he can help me find Joy again... If he can help me take her back home... I've got to try, and if it winds up costing me my soul or my life, I'm willing to risk it. I understood what that child meant when she said they all came here searching for something. I came here for a reason. I came here to find my Joy, and I'm not leaving without her. I know she's here; I've seen her with my own eyes... I've held her in my arms, for God's sake – I've felt her beating heart next to mine. She lives down here in this place. How could I know that and walk away? The answer is easy; I couldn't.

"I bade you tell me what you desire – now!" the creature's voice thunders down from the tree branches above me.

I quiet all thoughts of fear by picturing what the rest of my life without Joy in it would look like. No touch of her hand... no knowing glances from her eyes... no endless smiles upon her pretty face... making me feel alright... no nothing that means anything in the world to me... no commitment of marriage... no children of our own to hold onto... no life worthwhile living at all. That's what I've got to look forward to without her. It would be an emptier existence than the emptiness I saw in those pitiful children's eyes – a void ten times more hollow. I can't go back home carrying that broken parcel under my arm. I've got to answer Black Bobbin by telling the truth.

"I've come here to ask for your help," I manage to nervously push from my mouth.

"How can I help you, then, my little friend?" the half goat, half man smiles back his response.

I hardly know how I'm able, but I somehow continue to speak.

"I came to your world seeking someone I'd lost. I've found her here once but have since lost her. I need to find her again."

The creature stirs a bit closer, out from behind the trees. The shadows appear to cling to him rather than surround him. It's as though all the children are cowering at his feet.

He broadens his smile.

"I know the one you seek, Forrester, and I know you – just as I know everyone in this place. I know why you've come here. You're asking me to bring the dead back to life."

The children's song warned that he knows what lies inside your heart, so I guess there are no secrets here. And what's the difference? I just want him to help her.

The creature, now suddenly in front of me, shrinks down in size to more readily accommodate the company.

"Let's not get confused, now. You just want me to help you."

He can even read my mind. It seems there are no ends to what he's capable of doing.

"I do want her back more than anything. I don't deny that, but don't you think that she wants to live again?" I insist.

The horned creature chuckles.

"I believe she does, and yes, I can help you, for your little friend Joy lives down in these woods now. It is where she's come to rest."

"But she doesn't appear to be resting. She wanted me to follow her here. She wants to spend her life with me. I know it."

"No, she doesn't appear to be *resting*, as you like to put it. And yes, I believe she does, so I guess the question is what exactly are you asking me to do for you?"

He seems to be enjoying this far too much.

"I'm asking you to give her back to me – just like before... I want her to come home with me so we can spend our lives together."

The shrunken devil, who barely stands a foot above my head now, puts two fingers to his lips.

"Well, that's all fine and good, Forrester. I can do that for you, but what are you willing to give me in return?"

I've been waiting for that dreaded question. I knew it was the very thing he was bound to ask. I know I am willing to give him whatever he asks for. I am willing to sacrifice everything for the girl I love.

I look him straight in the eye – and try to prevent my knees from buckling.

"What do you want?"

The horned devil curls his smile half way round his head. Slow and slithering, it wraps its way into a toothy grin.

"I believe the question is more along the lines of, W*hat can you offer me?*"

I have to think about that for a moment... I know I would give him anything he asks, though I'm afraid of what it will be. I'm afraid it will involve giving up as much as I am gaining in return. I fear it will cost me everything I've got to give.

"I don't know what I've got that you could possibly want."

The creature chuckles slyly.

"Oh, I think you do."

I forgot; he appears to be able to read my mind. Still, I'm not quite sure what he truly wants from me. Judging by the lingering presence of the frightened children cowering around his feet and behind the nearby trees, I'm afraid he wants my soul, though I'm not even certain what that means.

"I don't know. I truly don't, but I'm willing to give you whatever you want – if you are able to do for me what I ask."

The creature's smile retracts a little.

"Trying to hide your true feelings won't work here, Forrester. Only the truth need bother passing between the two of us. Anything else is not worth the effort. I see into your thoughts and into your heart. I know exactly who you are and what you are thinking. You can't hide from me."

That's what I was afraid of. It definitely puts me at a disadvantage, for I certainly can't read his mind. However, I can see that there is no point trying to hide anything. Such a futile endeavour would only risk upsetting what I perceive already to be an extremely dangerous threat. I don't wish to poke a volatile bear with a lie-tipped stick. I have a feeling that it wouldn't work in my favour.

"I think you want to keep me here – just like the other children."

The creature throws its head back and laughs with such an intense force that it rattles the leaves off the trees above us.

"And you think that is too much to ask for what you are asking of me?"

"Well, no..." I falter, "but it would kind of defeat the purpose. I want to spend my days with Joy, not be apart from her."

"I understand what you want, my boy. However, don't you think I deserve a prize of equal value for my trouble? Shouldn't I receive something of similar worth in return?"

I hesitate slightly.

"...Yes, I suppose you do... I didn't mean to suggest you don't, but I really want to go home too so that Joy and I can be together."

The leathery black devil resumes smiling again.

"But you can go home. You can go home

any time you choose. I would be happy to show you the doorway that leads back to your world; however, unsettling to your ears as it may be, you must go home alone."

It is becoming quite clear to me that I'm not receiving the news I was hoping for.

"But that is not what I am asking of you. I want you to bring back my friend so that we can be together, and I want you to let us both go home."

The horned, foul-smelling beast looks upon me intently, his gaze gradually intensifying as though he's looking right through me.

"I know that it's not what you want to hear, Forrester, but only one of you can go home. You'll have to choose. I can bring her back... I can breath life into her again... I can send her back to your world – back to the time before she succumbed to her sickness... I can do all that if you wish, but I can't send you home together."

I can't prevent my heart from crashing all the way to my knees. It feels as though I'm losing Joy all over again. I'm losing heart in a hurry, for it feels like I'm losing everything.

"But why not?!" I plead, the vulgar desperation dripping from my lips ten times faster than I ever imagined possible. "Why can't you give me what I ask? I thought that you could do anything. Most of the animals here seem to think so."

The beast's chuckle is low and indulging.

"The animals here think what I want them to think. Everything in this world responds to my thoughts. Their only purpose was to bring you here. It's the only reason you encountered them at all. I just as easily could have hidden them from your eyes. I could have directed them elsewhere rather than into your path... However, they were right; I can do anything – but that doesn't mean it doesn't come at a cost. Everything comes at a cost, my young friend."

I find myself sinking to my knees, weighed down by tears.

"But the cost is too high! I'll still lose her!"

"But she'll live, Forrester... *She* will live. Will that not be worth it?"

With tears streaming down my cheeks like rivers through a canyon, I allow his words to settle in my brain. *She will live*... What a gift that would be to her – as well as me... knowing that she was alive and that I had given her that. I feel warmth in my heart just contemplating such an outcome, though I also feel loss – great loss that I wouldn't be there with her to enjoy it.

"Of course it would be worth it!" I thrust forth from my throat. "But why can't we be together? Why can't you give me that?"

The more I beg, the deeper my knees dig

their way into the ground.

The devil shrugs.

"Because that is not how it works, my friend. You can't expect something for nothing. If you give nothing, you receive nothing in return. If something is important enough to you, you must be willing to pay what it's worth. I'm only asking what is fair, no more."

I'm desperate now. I know he makes sense, but it doesn't do anything to make me feel better. My heart is still breaking. It doesn't change the fact that I won't have my Joy.

"But what if we both stay here? Can't you bring her back like before – after I found her down in the tunnels? Can't you give her back to me again – just as she was – and let us live out our lives together in this world? I'd be willing to do whatever you asked. I would serve you for the rest of my life if it meant having the chance to spend it with the girl I love."

The creature holding such power over me does his best to look sympathetic, though oddly, I seem able to see right through him.

"I am sorry, my son, but I'm afraid that's just not possible. Your little friend cannot live here. What you saw before was a ghost. She was nothing more than a ghost in your own mind. I know she seemed real, but she wasn't there at all. She cannot live in this world. She is very dead here."

I'm going out of my head with grief.

"But why did I see all the things that I did?! Why did I feel them?! They did feel real! How could they not be true? We talked together, I held her hand... she kissed me."

"I allowed you to see and feel them so that you would truly know what you were giving up."

I can't understand what he means.

"Giving up? But what was I giving up? You allowed me to see a life we hadn't lived – that we couldn't live... unless we were permitted to return home together."

The creature smiles softly.

"It was the life you would have lived if she had not died. It was important for you to experience that... to truly know what you had lost. It was the only way for you to know if you were willing to pay the price of what you're asking for – to know if her life is worth your own."

I'm desperate and confused and bleeding tears into the ground.

"But how can one be worth more than the other? How can either be worth anything without the other?"

"The question, my friend, is which one is worth more to you."

The silence trailing off the end of his words leaves me with no recourse but to ponder the full extent of the numbness settling into my heart.

"If I stay behind, will I still be able to see her – in my head like before, I mean? Will it at least still seem real to me?"

The shaking of his head from side to side strips even that slim shred of hope away.

"I'm afraid not, Forrester. Once she returns to your world, all that will be lost. You will not see her again. I will no longer be able to conjure her ghost. It's only while she's buried down here that I have the power to awake such thoughts in your mind."

That surprises me; I thought I'd at least have that much.

"But I thought that you could do anything! I was under the impression there was nothing out of your reach."

"I'm sorry, Forrester, but it doesn't work that way. I only hold dominion down here. I can breath life into your little friend and send her back to your world, but beyond that, I have no control over anything that happens there. And once gone, she will be as lost to me as she is to you. You won't be able to see her, and I won't be able to help you. No, Forrester, if you give her up, I'm afraid you'll be giving her up for good. If you choose to give her life, you're letting go of her completely. It's how it has to be. You need to know that."

The creature licks at his pointy yellow finger nails, which more closely resemble claws.

"So, what is it going to be, my young friend. A decision has got to be made."

I stare haphazardly at the hole in the sky above me. Not enough light can possibly penetrate the ruin inside my heart. What am I going to do? Of course if there's a chance, I want Joy to live again... but I am giving up so much. I know I truly would give up anything to have her back again and to spend my life with her... The not being with her is the part I'm having trouble with. I don't know if I can stand never seeing her again. It might be far too detrimental to my heart.

"Can you not give me more time to think it over?" I find myself practically begging.

There is a smile half awakening beneath his placid stare – one I'm not exactly sure I'm comfortable with.

"Time is all you humans concern yourselves with in your world. You never think you have enough time, but time is all you really have... until it runs out on you, that is. Then that is it. You are all limited editions, whether you like it or not. In this world, time doesn't appear to exist. Everything stays pretty much the same, with no obvious changes to mark any kind of progress forward, so what else are our inhabitants to believe? To them, every moment feels exactly like the one before it... until they disappear. The others are aware of their absence, but with no obvious indication that anything else has changed, they immediately doubt their memories. They easily dismiss them as no more than a clever idea in their heads or a fond yearning for something different. Much too easily they forget that they were ever there at all and things continue to go on as though time never existed. Really though, time is all there is here as well. An endless parade of silence awaits them like anywhere else. Whether you're marking changes on a calendar or watching one moment mirror the last, it makes no difference; you are here until you're not. When your time is up, you disappear. So, can I give you more time, you ask me? Well, you'll have to be the judge of that... Perhaps there is a little."

I don't know why I'm finding it so hard to make the decision. I was quite content to die rather than go through life without her, yet I believe I somehow hoped I'd be with her then, in heaven or wherever we go after we've breathed our last. If I agree to this, I won't get to see her at all. She'll be lost to me forever – any real connection I have left. I will be without the one who knows my heart best. How can I possibly agree to such a final resolution? It would be the equivalent of sacrificing my heart. However, I know I'm willing to do it... if it means giving Joy another chance at life. I've made up my mind. I turn to the black bearded devil, who has been patiently stroking his chin.

"If you give me more time here with Joy –

allow the two of us to be together again, I'll be able to make up my mind."

The creature chuckles.

"You forget, Forrester. I know what you're thinking. I know you will give me what I want. But yes, I will do as you ask. I can give you that much. I will give you one day with her – as it would feel in your world, but at the end, you'll have to choose, though I know you already have. It just won't be easy, that's all. It will be the hardest thing you've ever had to do. So I have to ask you, are you sure you don't want to cut ties now and come under my protection? Your little friend can go back to your world to live again, and you can become one of my children and serve me as the others do."

The children cowering about the creature's feet poke their heads out – one after another in a nauseous rhythm, flashing their wide eyes and chalk bone grins. Black Bobbin's form once more begins to rise in height and stature, reaching further into the trees with every word.

"In exchange for your simple pledge of loyalty and obedience... in return for you agreeing to do a few menial chores around the place, I will grant you all your desires but one – you will never see your friend again. If you can accept that, you can have whatever you want all the time, and you'll feel as though you'll live forever. Come to terms with the one thing you desire the most and this place can be your oasis."

The foul fragranced animal stands ten feet tall again, its limbs and hooves growing stout with every added rise, sending the low-mouthed children scurrying in all directions. He takes such time with his words to make it all sound so near to being wonderful... if only I can give up the one thing that truly would. I believe he does know my thoughts – and at the very least, my heart. He already knows what I'll do – perhaps more than I know it myself. Perhaps he's known all along. Even before his whispers reached the rabbits' ears, I'm sure he was onto me. I'm sure it was why he brought me here.

"Give me one day. That's all I ask. You already know that I'll give you what you want."

"Yes, we both know that I do, Forrester, so let us consider this offering an act of faith. Consider it a great favour – a sentimental gift of love from my old heart to yours, my boy."

The ache in the pit of my stomach gives me every cause to doubt his motives – certainly substantial reason to question him being in possession of such a gifted organ as a heart. I know he's taking everything I could possibly give him. He's taking everything I have... and in return he's offering the one thing I can't refuse. No, it's quite clear what he is after. He's out to get but one thing from me – my poor battered and broken soul. I'm very close to thinking that he is the devil and I am in hell. This is the underworld I've fallen into, and I've pretty much accepted that I am never going to get out.

Black Bobbin shrinks back down to my size once more and reaches out a bony hand.

"Let us shake on it, then, Forrester. It seems we have a deal done."

I hesitate back a bit before proceeding.

"I accept what you are so graciously, kind and generously offering; however, my word will not be final until the day is through. Only then will I make my choice, though knowing what you know, I'm sure you believe you have nothing to worry about."

The gnarled, claw tipped hand retracts faster than a rattler striking at the flesh of a barking dog.

"So be it, my lovely son. So be it that you may have all the choices in the world. I'll give you what you ask and wait for your decision. I've got no question in my mind that in the end, we'll both wind up with what we truly want."

The creature's stale laughter wraps around the trees and swirls above me as he shrinks away out of sight. All that's left are his children's shadows, creeping slowly back into the scarce light. It feels as though they mean to harm me, for they encircle me completely, forming an airtight ring that leaves my heart rigid and my lungs feeling twice as tight. Once more their singing tries to lull me off to somewhere I'd rather not go.

"Black Bobbin... Black Bobbin... He's a

wily old goat. He grazes in the forest and helps us when he can, and all we have to do in return is offer out our hands. Black Bobbin... Black Bobbin... We do all he asks. We toil when he wishes and are submissive when he yells. We know better not to cross him, for then we truly would be trapped in hell."

The children's harsh singing leaves blisters in my ears. Their words don't exactly paint their *kindly* benefactor in a charitable light. They make him sound more like the trickster devil I suspect him to be. I guess there is no sense in hiding it; I already know as much on my own accord. I'm quite aware that he's trying to trap me here. It's obvious that they're afraid of him, as I should be myself. I am afraid of him. There is no question strong enough to deny the merit behind those words. I don't trust him one bit, and he gives me the creeps, for good measure. My skin is still crawling from our conversation. But what could I do? He didn't leave me with much of a choice. If I didn't agree to humour him and at least consider his terms, he might have killed me – at worst, and at best, not allowed me the opportunity to see Joy again. He certainly wouldn't have given me the option of saving her. And what would that have left me with? I'd still be trapped here. I'd be lost and alone and wandering around, just waiting to stumble into my next pitfall. My chances of surviving here without any help are slim to none. Since he controls the animals, they wouldn't be able to help me on their own. He might even force them to turn on me and do me in. Giant moles and rabbits could join the killer fish and birds of prey to hunt me down and murder me. I'm sure I'd make a lovely meal for some hungry beast.

The way those orphan kids are eyeing me up, I'd swear that they have similar thoughts in mind. They look pretty gaunt for ones prone to receiving whatever they want from their master. Spending an eternity of moments – one stretched out after the next – in their company doesn't sound too appealing. I'd be afraid to close my eyes to try to sleep for worry that I'd awake to the sound of them gnawing through the flesh of my leg. It makes me wonder if I'd be treated with similar neglect.

"Scram!" I yell at my tormentors, causing them to evaporate as quickly as Black Bobbin escaped upon the wind. Into the shadows they sink without resistance. It happens so fast that I'm not certain if they merely step behind trees or vanish into the thinness of the air. I guess it doesn't matter, though I wonder what it says about their authenticity to truth. Are they real, or are they too only imagined? And what does that say about my chances here?

CHAPTER 13

THE AUTHENTICITY OF THE EXPERIENCE

Some things have a way of sneaking up on you even when you're expecting them. I believe Black Bobbin. I believe he will let me see Joy again. I'm just not sure about the specifics or how exactly it is going to take place.

It turns out I don't have to trouble my thoughts for long. I am presented with the answer forthwith. It's not dramatic. She doesn't descend down from the heavens on a beam of light or rise up out of a crack in the earth. No, the subtle approach appears to be the preferred method of choice – be it Black Bobbin's or my own... or be it hers. I might only be imagining it, but he's apparently the one making it all happen. I might be the one who is dreaming, but he's making my dreams come true. He's allowing me to see and hear and feel something very close to being real. So near to it, in fact that I don't recognize it as being anything else. It feels just about as real as real can be, and if I can forget that I know any different, it will be real to me. So as I look up to see my favourite girl in the whole wide world of Oz standing there between two trees, as though she's been in that special place all along, I am less shocked than relieved by such a favourable outcome. She wasn't there and now she is, as radiant and beautiful as a wild orchid in bloom. She's wearing a yellow cotton sundress beneath a burgundy shawl. Her soft, silky blonde hair is falling about her shoulders and face in ringlets, and the pout on her cherry red lips is providing the perfect contrast to the solemn mood. Forget that I might never see her again after today; I've got everything that I could possibly want right in this moment.

As soon as she lays eyes on me, I can feel the authenticity of the experience. She is here with me now, just as real as ever – as real as before when we escaped from the tunnel... as real as when we fell into the swamp... as real as all my days spent with her back home. What else am I to believe other than that she is present? The way she is looking at me sells the story for everything it's worth. I can see it in her eyes; she misses me... I can see the pain she's suffering from us being torn apart... I can see the depths of the loss in her heart. She knows every bit as much as I do what's been lost. Words need not bother our thoughts for the moment; we're too busy running into each other's arms. As much as I wanted it to happen, I wasn't sure whether I would ever see her again, and I sense, somehow, that she felt the same. It is clear that we both feel extremely blessed to be standing where we are right now. Holding onto one another tightly and staring into each other's eyes, she states it plainly.

"I never want to be apart from you again. Please promise never to let me go."

With tears welling in my own, clouding my better judgment, I falter with the truth. Though how could I do any different? I don't want to ever let her go, and if I do, I know it is going to have to be sudden; I can't imagine the kind of strength it would take to say goodbye.

"I won't... I will hold onto you forever," are the words I choose as compensation.

Along with the overwhelming sense of relief and gratefulness pouring over my bones for being granted this belated reunion, I'm in agony over knowing it is not meant to last. All I wish to do is tune it out and run away with the girl who means so very much to me – to my sanity... to my sense of who I am. I'm sure I'm in denial but perhaps that is the best possible place for me to be right now; it will delay my impending death from grief.

"Come with me!" I beg of her. "We need to get away from this place. We will head back up to higher ground – closer to the sunshine. I'm sure if we can get out of these trees, we'll stand a better chance of finding a way back home."

"I'll follow you anywhere," she confides through quivering lips. "Just promise you will always be there."

"I'll always be there," I tell her, only half admitting the truth.

I'll be there as much as she's able to hold fast to the memory. I will always be there in that sense – as a fading piece of parchment in her head, so it's not a complete scrap of dishonesty; it's partly the truth.

"Let's go then!" I declare. "Let's leave this dark place behind and find the sunshine. Let us find all the beautiful things a day of adventure holds. We'll make this a day for exploring. Who knows what we'll find in a place like this."

Secretly, in my heart, I'm hoping it will be some way to escape back home. Part of me is still clinging to the delusion that everything Black Bobbin told me is a lie. I want to believe that I'm seeing Joy because she is real. I don't want to believe that she can't stay here or that we can't both return home together. That same part inside of me can't accept that she will have to leave when this day ends... that I will have to make a choice – a choice harder than I ever thought I'd have to make. I don't want to think about any of it right now. If this truly is the last day I've been given to spend with Joy, I'm not going to waste it. I'm going to hang onto it for all that it's worth... savour every moment, for it might be all I have to get me through the rest.

Taking her hand in mine, I lead her away from all the shadows. Tree after tree, we pass and mark as history. Never looking back, we forge ahead. I pray I'll never have to see that ugly goat, Black Bobbin, again. Perhaps he was the thing imagined – the scariest spectre possible that I could conjure inside my head... to offer me a terrible ultimatum... the perfect scenario to bring to life my darkest fears. I know I want to exorcise all thoughts of him from my head this very moment. I want to focus on the gift I'm holding onto with my hand.

Joy is wearing a white dress the colour of soft lilies. It's ruffled and pleated, with puffy sleeves. She looks like an absolute angel, she is so beautiful, though it's not a dress she used to wear. It is the dress they buried her in... My troubled mind races back to catch up to the memory of her little casket being lowered deep beneath the hill. I'm struggling with what that says about the here and now.

Gazing over at her, I try not to let my worried eyes spoil the moment. I'm doing my best to keep a smile upon my lips and a look of tender optimism on my face.

"Remember all the days we spent exploring the woods behind Cabot's Hill – all the tunnels through the rocks and hollow trees across silver streams... Remember lying atop the soft maple grass with bare arms and legs, looking up at the endless blue ocean of sky above us. We dreamt of life to come... We dreamt of the life that we'd have one day... We dreamt about everything."

"I remember," she tells me softly. "I remember all of it – every beautiful day together... every playful swirl of laughter... every tender kiss."

Her kisses I will always miss... They were the innocent kisses of children, but they were filled with love. My heart aches for all the kisses lost through losing her... the ones I will never know.

I can't help turning to Joy to beg a favour.

"Kiss me..." I insist. "I want to know what it feels like to kiss you for real."

Her bright blue eyes agree without her words bothering to make the effort. She steps towards me, and I pull her in. Pressed tightly against my body, holding her firmly, I place my lips on hers. The moist anticipation of what will happen next fills my senses with rejuvenation. I feel as though we can finally continue from the place where we left off. I felt something of it down in the tunnel, though there seems much more urgency in this moment than ever before. Things feel more real in the here and now than they could possibly feel behind a thin veil of a future that does not exist. Today, I want to experience everything deeply. If this is the last day we have together, I want to squeeze out every drop... of sunshine, laughter – and especially, love... I don't want my lips to ever part from this girl's mouth. I don't want my arms to fall away from holding her close. I always want to hear the sweet music of her soul filling my senses. I want to live today as though it were one beautiful, perfect moment, one that is equivalent to a lifetime, for it very well could be all we have left. I don't want my lips to falter. I continue to press them tightly against her precious skin.

All the stars erupt across the sky in desperation, for they're well aware of what I might be giving up inside my heart. They are no longer hiding themselves behind the daylight. They're shining on in spite of the lack of night. Joy and I need to be like those stars above us. We mustn't allow a lack of anything to hold us back.

We continue on up the mountain – with every step, getting nearer to the sky. As we get higher, the trees push their presence closer to the horizon. They seem damned determined to completely block out the sun.

"I don't know how these animals can live in such darkness," Joy questions. "Is there no place capable of shedding more light?"

I pause for a moment to shrug my shoulders.

"Everything in this forest appears to be shrouded in a kind of darkness. This whole world seems to be smothered by trees. However, there has got to be someplace that lets in the sunshine. Perhaps if we can find such a place, we will find someone who can help us."

I turn to face her firmly.

"Know that I haven't given up, Joy. I won't stop searching for a way out of here. There must be some way to get us back to Cabot's Hill."

"Cabot's Hill..." Her whisper trails off, leaving her looking a little lost. "Yes, back home to Cabot's Hill. It's where we live... where we grew up."

Her movement within the present improving

little, she continues.

"I know the place, Forrester. I remember..."

"That's good, Joy. You had me worried for a moment. I wasn't sure where you had gone to."

The lovely girl can only smile; she doesn't seem to know what else to say.

We climb further up the rock cut paths, which line the steep like jagged rungs upon a ladder. I hold Joy tightly by her hand, pulling her nearer to the top of the hill with every carefully laboured step. Eventually, we think we've reached the summit, only to have closer inspection reveal that it's no more than a plateau. Disappointed as we are in knowing that our journey must continue on, we are relieved to have a rest. We are pleased to find a place with grass absent of tree trunks stabbing down into the earth.

"It is a fine patch of grass to have a rest on," Joy invites me in her soft, sweet asking voice.

"Yes," I agree, "it looks like the best place to sit down that I've seen in a while. I think we should take a break here before climbing the rest of the way up the hillside. I only wish we had some food."

My stomach is starting to rumble. It seems so long ago that I ate at the strawberry patch.

Joy has the most peculiar of looks upon her

pretty face.

"It's odd, but I'm not hungry. I suppose I ought to be; it must be ages since I've eaten."

That worries me; she should be hungry, though what can I do but dismiss it with all the rest. Instead, I try to reassure her.

"Don't worry about it. I'm sure your appetite will return once we get out of this place. I know that my stomach has been unsettled since my arrival here."

The sweet girl tries a half smile.

"I hope so, Forrester. You know how I used to love to eat."

I do better and make the effort fully.

"I know, Joy. I know... We both did."

Hunger is gnawing at my guts, but the last thing I want to do is rub it in. Instead, I will subdue both our worried hearts and entirely forget the relief that food could bring.

"Oh well, let's content ourselves with rest. It will feel good to get off our tired legs for a while and nestle down into that patch of tall, soft grass."

We move towards the centre of the little clearing, quite aware that there is scarcely more light above us. The treetops around us have simply moved over to fill the space in. Just when we think we've reached the perfect spot, a step further forward reveals what we've fallen into. The seemingly solid pack of grass gives way suddenly, sending both Joy and I tumbling down into a deep, bowl-like impression in the ground. Still struggling with the shock of losing all stability, we're quick to realize we're not alone. Something soft, warm and fluffy provides a cushion to land against.

CHAPTER 14

A NEST FULL OF KITTENS

It's hard to get the words out for sheer surprise, but opening my eyes a little wider shows the truth. It appears we've landed in a nest of kittens – or a basket full of them, or something just as neat. The little cats aren't so little; they're nearly the size of us. The two of us are more shocked than frightened. It's hard to be intimidated by something so cute – and once they start licking our faces, about all that's left to do is giggle. There are five of them in total – two whites, one orange, a tabby and one black as soot. The orange and tabby are fluffier than the other three, which have shinier, sleeker bodies that would be sure to glisten in the sun. It's strange cuddling with a kitten the size of myself. It is more like a friendly wrestling match than anything else. If the gentle creatures took the notion, they could maul us just as easily as snuggle up close. Even if only in play, it could happen. I had better not allow myself to be lulled into a false sense of calm. Danger often lurks in tranquil settings, behind smiles and on front porch steps. These cute, fluffy kittens might be hungry. They might see us as their next meal and only be licking us to soften us up for a feeding. If they wanted to, they could take a bite out of us the size of a baseball with those strong jaws of theirs. I think we'd be wise to get out of this hole before we find out which way the truth is leaning.

I push two of the kittens away from me and grab Joy by her arm.

"C'mon, Joy, we'd better get out of here; it might not be safe."

She seems in no hurry to vacate the premises.

"Aw, but they're so cute! Can't we stay and cuddle with them a little longer? I miss my cat, Persia, so much."

"I know they're cute. They're adorable, in fact, but they are the size of us! They could kill us if they wanted to – or at least, hurt us pretty good. We can't be taking those kinds of chances; it is the surest way of seeing ourselves killed!"

Joy looks disappointed but nods in agreement. I pull her away from the tabby, and we both stand up awkwardly on the soft grass floor. We're just about to try crawling up out of the repressed cereal bowl we find ourselves in when a familiar voice startles us from above.

"I see you've met my offspring."

I look up to see Jackson Trigg standing on the lip of the hollow staring down at us. He is shaking his head.

"Would you be so kind as not to disturb them. They view you as new play toys. The last thing I need is for them to become spoiled and want humans of their own."

I apologize promptly, surprisingly happy to see the big white cat.

"I am very sorry. We fell into their bed by accident. We were climbing up the hillside and just wanted a comfortable place to rest."

The fat white feline looks suspicious.

"And where would you be heading with such conviction in your eyes, my fine young friend? Are you still in search of things you cannot have? Hm, still trying to make the impossible possible?"

I am tired of hearing nothing but negativity out of Jackson's mouth.

"If you mean, am I still trying to find a way home, then yes, I continue on that most futile of quests."

I can feel the sympathy in his gaze.

"As I've told you before, you can go home at any time. All you have to do is accept why you've come here."

I'm tired of the cat's patronizing tone.

"And as I've told you before, I've come here to find Joy, and I'm not leaving without her – and if you can't help me with that, I have no need of your company."

"It is not that I don't want to help you, Forrester, but I can't help you do the impossible. I know you've been to see the witch of the forest – that old goat, Black Bobbin himself."

"And what of it?" I protest in defiance.

"I know what he's offered you, that he's made you believe your little friend is still here with you, and even more outlandish, that he can make her live again. I know it's not what you wanted, but he knows as well as I do that anything is better than nothing inside your broken heart."

He speaks the truth; I am so desperate to have her back again that I'd grab at just about anything right now.

"So what if it is? I can't help it; I love her too much."

I see great sadness in the cat's large eyes as he lowers his gaze towards the ground.

"I know you do, Forrester, and that's why it's far too easy for you to be taken in. Do you really think that he's going to keep his word? Do you really think he can make Joy live again?"

Honestly, I don't know what to think about anything right about now.

"I thought he could do anything."

Jackson frowns.

"And why would you think that?"

I have to think about that for a moment.

"It's what the other animals and the children of the forest said."

"And who do you suppose puts words in their mouths?"

"But we made a deal... If I give him what he wants, he has to keep his word," I protest.

The big cat's whiskers are twitching so much that I can't see how he's managing to refrain from laughing out loud.

"You foolish child. As soon as you give him what he wants, he doesn't have to do anything – and he won't! He'll have you exactly where he wants you. You'll be trapped here under his power, just like those other poor lost souls. He's the reason you've come here. He's the one who drew you down here, not the girl. He simply showed you what you wanted to see, and he's still doing it. Joy is dead, Forrester. She is still buried deep beneath the ground. What you're seeing is not real – it's not true."

"Don't you think I know that?" I grumble. "He's told me as much. He's explained how it works... how he's only allowing me to see those things but that doesn't mean he can't bring her back to life again. If I agree to stay here, he has promised to give her her life back."

Jackson Trigg's smile is complete.

"That is very noble of you, Forrester... If only you could trust a devil such as him."

The longer he gazes upon me, the more I can see the sympathy growing in his eyes.

"You need to know that he only holds dominion down here. He has no power in your world. In this dark forest, he can manipulate your senses, thoughts, memories... He can make anyone appear to come back to life. However, as soon as they cross that threshold and step back into the place you know as home, his authority ends. Putting my words as plainly as possible, so as not to suffocate your ears, if your little friend is dead in your world now, she will stay dead. He nor anyone else can bring her back to life and that is the sad truth of the matter. He lied to you, Forrester. All he wants to do is keep you here. That is why he has lured you to this place. He collects the souls of lost children."

I know that Jackson Trigg is only telling me the things I don't want to be hearing, though deep down believe to be true. However, it still leaves me feeling miserable to hear them. There is little in his words to offer reassurance – certainly not the sort I wish to hear.

"And why should I believe you? You haven't done much to help me. He's the only one who's offered me anything at all. Why wouldn't I accept his help? Where else can I turn?! Who else is going to help me?! What are you willing to do for me? You haven't offered me anything that I want!"

The large cat's conviction is unwavering.

"I've offered you the truth."

"It's not the truth that I want to hear!" I bark up at him from the depression in the ground I'm stuck in.

Jackson Trigg appears unmoved by my outburst.

"It is exactly what you need to hear, Forrester. It's why I'm here; it is my duty to guide you."

"Why are you here?!" I yell at him. "What is your true purpose? Why aren't your thoughts controlled by Black Bobbin like everyone else's down here? Or maybe they are! Perhaps you're working with him too. Why should I trust you any more than anyone else? What places you atop such hallowed ground?"

The conviction in the cat's voice comes across truer than ever before.

"I'm the only one here who can help you. I'm the only one who is outside Black Bobbin's reach. He holds no power over me. My role here is to counterbalance all the harm he does. In all places there exists someone or something to even things out. Even in our world there has to be balance.

Without it, nothing could last."

I don't understand and it's frustrating me to no ends.

"Then, why won't you help me?!" I bemoan, nearly on the verge of tears.

"I have been helping you, Forrester. You've been too blinded by your grief to see it, that's all."

"All you've done is try to take my hope away. You've asked me to accept the one thing I cannot accept. I don't want to accept that Joy is dead. I want to believe she can be brought back to life..."

I turn to look upon Joy, still standing beside me, faithfully holding onto my hand.

"I want to believe that what I am seeing is real."

Jackson Trigg shakes his head in an apologetic manner.

"I am sorry, Forrester, but I'm not going to lie to you. I don't see her there. Only you perceive her presence to be true."

His honesty comes at a cost – my disappointment.

"Well, she appears real to me and that is all that really matters, I suppose. Why can't I just stay here and be with her always? If what you say is true and Joy cannot be brought back to life again in my world, then, Black Bobbin should be able to make it so that I can be with her for the remainder of my life – even if it is only in my head. Why wouldn't he do that if I agree to stay here and serve him?"

The big cat unravels a precious frown.

"He could do it – if he wanted to, but he won't... because he doesn't have to. Once he gets what he wants, he won't be doing you any favours, know that. You will be nothing more than a slave to him, and you'll be stuck here for good – and you have no idea how long a lifetime lasts in our world. Living such a miserable existence, catering to that black devil's every whim, will feel like an eternity – one you don't want to know."

"I believe you; I fully expect it will be miserable, but what I don't understand is why won't he simply allow me to keep the visions in my head – just let me keep seeing her? Why would he offer me something he can't make good on?"

"Because he knows you want more."

The cat is right; as much as I am grateful to be experiencing thoughts so lucid that it feels like Joy is really here. If I truly don't believe she's real, I know that there will come a time where it's not enough. I will want more – and breathing life back into Joy's lungs to allow her to live again would mean more to me than anything. Although I want to be with her as desperately as a heart can ache for something, a second chance for her would be worth so much more. I believe that Black Bobbin does know that. He knows he had to offer me something that felt painfully real. He knows I needed to be faced with a terrible choice.

Jackson Trigg's logic is only proving to confuse me more. I'm beginning to doubt my chances of seeing any kind of worthwhile outcome.

"Well, what exactly would you have me do, then?" I complain. "I can't just walk away. I can't give up as long as there is any shred of hope at all... unless you can offer me something more. Please, I'm begging you! Give me a reason!"

With obvious compassion in his voice, the large white cat gives me my answer.

"I'm afraid I can't give you what you want, Forrester. I wish I could, but I won't lie to you. The best I can do is guide you towards finding your own way home and back to your family. I will show you the way, but you have to choose to walk it. I can't do it for you."

I know I'm being difficult, but, forgive me; I can't help it.

"And I suppose that would involve accepting that Joy is dead and walking away from her."

"I am sorry, Forrester, but you must accept that your friend is gone. If you don't, you will never leave here."

That ultimatum is put about as bluntly as can be. If I can't leave behind my heart... if I don't abandon the one who means everything to me, I will never leave this place, but of course, I already knew that – if I believed anything that Black Bobbin said was truth. There's just no guarantee that Joy can be helped either way and that is the most disheartening thing in the world to me.

"I can't do that," I force from my lips dryly, taking more than I've got at the moment to say anything at all. "I won't do that. I would rather be stuck here for good than walk away from her... I would rather die."

The sad tone of his voice won't be outdone by the heartbreaking look in his eyes.

"It has always been your choice to make, Forrester. Just remember, you can choose different."

With that, the big white cat swings around to face the other way, dropping his tail down into the hole in the process.

"Grab hold and I'll pull you up," he instructs strictly. "Our kittens need to feed, and they are growing weary of the wait. You've lingered here too long."

Turning to look behind me, I can see that all five kittens are squirming impatiently and increasingly tightening their still closed eyes. No sooner do I discover their anxiety than they begin to cry out for their mother.

I risk a dumb question and ask, "Is there a Mrs. Trigg?"

Jackson spreads his smile across his mouth slyly.

"Yes, she'll be along shortly. You'd best not let her find you here, for she won't take too kindly to you disturbing her children, and I'm afraid I won't be able to help you; I'm not fool enough to stand between a mother and her young."

I look over at Joy to see that she is still with me. She might only be in my head, but so far, Black Bobbin's word seems to be holding up. To me anyways, she appears as real as real can be. And seeing her lovely face smiling back at me and feeling the subtle warmth of her hand, how can I believe her to be anything else?

"C'mon, Joy, grab hold. We have to get going. We must get to the top of the hill. We've got to find a way out of here. There has to be some way to get home."

As always, she trusts me without hesitation, though at the moment, I fear I shouldn't be trusted at all. I'm in no position to promise anything; I'm the last one to know what our survival will take. I wonder how she could hear Jackson's words and not be completely frightened to death. His insistence that she is dead and not really here has got to weigh heavy on her heart. Hearing that she can never hope for anything more surely must leave the emptiest of space. I wish I could have protected her from hearing such obvious words of pain. I wish I could have protected her from it all. I'm sure she must understand, though she's too brave to show it. She's not letting on that the weight of her heart being crushed is holding her down. Her smile is as full of Joy as ever. She's positively beaming as we're both pulled up to level ground by one firm swish of the big cat's tail.

"We must part company here," Jackson purrs warmly. "I wish you well, my young friend. I pray you choose wisely. I know it is the most difficult decision you've ever had to make."

I nod to the sleek bodied white Spinx to acknowledge my sense of understanding before returning to the one thing we've got left to ground us. The best thing we can do right now is stay focused and the surest way to do that is to find our way back up to higher ground, where hopefully we might find a doorway out of this world.

As we work our way towards the massive stand of trees glaring down at us from atop the ridge, I keep looking back at Joy, who is one step behind me still holding onto my hand. I'm trying to judge her mood, her moral equilibrium... her willingness to continue. I feel I should say something; although, I'm very aware that, at the moment, silence might be the most calming presence of all. In spite of my uneasy manner, I decide to chance it and ask Joy if she is alright.

"I hope that what the cat said isn't bothering you. I don't believe him, I want you to know. I believe in my heart that you are very real and very much alive. I know you are here. I can touch and feel you. I can see you with my own two eyes. I know we can find our way home. We just have to keep searching, that's all. There has got to be a way. I just know there is. And just as long as you don't let go of my hand, I won't lose you. We've got to hang onto each other tightly this time so that we won't get parted again. We must stay close together until we can find a way out of this place. Trust me, Joy. Both of us will make it home, and we can spend our lives together... just like we've always wanted... just like it was meant to be."

Just as soon as I let the words *trust me* slip out of my mouth, I knew I was playing loosely with the truth, and I feel guilty for having said it. I have no way of knowing whether the two of us will make it home together. All signs point so far to the contrary, in fact, that only a fool would believe otherwise. Well, better to be a fool than a boldfaced liar. That way, at least, it would mean I still believed there was some hope. I'm not even sure if one of us will ever get the chance to walk up Cabot's Hill again. According to the devil goat, Joy will only make it home if I stay behind. Jackson Trigg claims that I'm the only one who can possibly leave. I don't know who I am to believe – or what... or why any of this is happening. Why was I brought here at all if Joy and I can't be together? Why was I drawn into this world just to face disappointment and heartache? What was the point of all that?

As though reading my mind... as always, so near to my thoughts, Joy cheers me up a little.

"Don't worry so much about finding a way home, Forrester. We are together right now. Let's enjoy this time. I mean, aren't we blessed to have found each other in this place – amidst this strange world, so far from our home? Shouldn't we enjoy it?"

She has always known just what to say to make me smile, though her words could just as easily bring me to tears.

"Of course we should. It's a beautiful day. We've got each other. What more do we truly need? Let's not waste another moment on worry or unappreciative thought. Let's find the sunshine. Let's be thankful for all the blessings we've got."

My beautiful friend is grinning from ear to ear – so much that my own heart can't desist from melting.

"I am, Forrester. I am so happy to know we are together."

Fighting back my purging tears, I tighten my sentences to get my words out completely.

"C'mon, then, once we get to the top of this rise, the sky can't be far off. If we can find our way out of this forest, anything is possible."

We each hand our smile over to the other to

warm our hearts more thoroughly and allow the positive energy to carry us the rest of the way up the hill. We reach the summit without hardly noticing, for we keep walking without bothering to stop. The air seems fresher up here, the light a little less dark.

"Which way should we go?" I ask Joy, hoping that she has a better sense of direction than I do, not bothering to accept the fact that she might not actually be here. She's far too real to me to consider anything different, and truth be told, I don't want to think about it; I just want to enjoy having her here right now, hold onto what I've got in this moment, the exact precious allotment of time – however long that might be.

"Why not this way?" my favourite girl asks with an encouraging smile.

I think it's the way I came in, but why not? Perhaps it's the way out of here too.

"Sounds good to me. It looks as fine a way as any. I'm sure it will lead us out of these woods."

We strike forth with vigour, walking as fast as we can, and before we know it, we seem to be getting somewhere new and complete. The darkness appears to be thinning out around us. Closer observation reveals the reason for it. The trees are thinning out to keep pace. I can't help feeling exited and want Joy to share in the enthusiasm.

"I think we're nearing the edge of the forest. There are far fewer trees here. Look at all the sunshine. It is like an entirely new place."

"Yes, it's very beautiful. Everything looks so vibrant and green all of a sudden. I am so glad to be spending the day here with you."

I return the sentiment immediately, without hesitation.

"And I with you."

I give her a hug to make everything feel a little more real, and we continue on with a rejuvenated spring in our steps. We were not mistaking; we have definitely found our way out of the woods. Often, we think we're gaining ground when we're really falling backwards, and, sometimes, when we think we've gotten ahead, all we've truly done is lost track of time. I should have known that today life would be no different. Just when we think the darkness is behind us, a new shadow casts its way down from the truth. A strange music starts playing – the kind cranked out of a wind up music box that you'd see at a circus or a fair... the candied carnival kind that creeps you out and excites you all at the same time. As we move forward into this new realm of sound, we bring the denseness of the forest back with us. The trees wrap their grappling limbs around us as though we never left. I can't even claim we're in a clearing; we are lost in the woods as much as before.

CHAPTER 15

A CARNIVAL IN THE FOREST

Looking at each other awkwardly, it's quite plain to see that we're both uncertain whether we ought to go forward, but really, what else can we do? The forest appears to have closed up behind us. I can't even see a pathway back the way we came in.

"What's happening?" Joy reaches out with a question to something we'd both like to know.

"I'm not sure. I'm as confused as you are, but it appears we weren't on the edge of the forest at all."

"Where was all the sunlight coming from, then?" the sweet little girl begs me to know.

"It must have been a thinning out of the trees, nothing more. It was just wishful thinking on our parts to believe any different. However, we mustn't lose hope. If we keep moving forward, there is no reason we won't find a way out of here yet. In the meantime, this place looks interesting enough. Who would have thought we'd find a carnival in the forest? That's what this is, you know. Look, there are games and rides – and can't you smell the popcorn and candy floss up ahead?"

Looking around us, the little girl can't argue no different.

"You're right, Forrester; it is a carnival, though how can it be in such a place as this?"

"If I've learned anything since my arrival here, it is that anything is possible in this world. We just have to go with it and accept it as a matter of fact. It's unlike anything that we're used to back home. It's why I believe we're able to exist here... It is why I believe we are bound to find a way home."

Joy throws her arms around me in delight.

"I know we are blessed to be here together. Let's enjoy the gift of this day as though it were our last."

If only she knew how accurate her words could turn out to be, though I don't want to think about the horrible truth of the matter. I wish for nothing more than to enjoy whatever time we might have.

"Yes, let us do just that. Let's go on all the rides, play all the games and stuff our faces until we can't stand the sight of all that junk. It will be just like when we were little children. It was where we first met... at the fair."

The lovely girl smiles as though she's bending pure sunlight and the resulting warmth takes me back eight summers ago.

"I remember. It was on The Ferris Wheel. You were afraid to ride on it alone."

"You're right; I believe I was," I tell her. "But you were willing to sit beside me, and you held my hand and soothed me, just like you've always done... and I've loved you for it ever since."

"I know you have, and I've loved you and that is why I brought you here. I had to be with you again, for all I've done is miss you."

Holding her in the softness of my eyes, I can't help but cry. I knew it was her who brought me here. I knew she wouldn't leave me alone. She could see that my heart was breaking... She could see how thoroughly I missed her touch.

"When I left you up on Cabot's Hill, I never thought I'd see you again. I thought I had lost you for good. For weeks, I searched all the places we used to go for some sign – for any sign of you. You were everywhere, lingering in all the spaces in between – in the trees, the grass, the hills and haunted ruins where we used to play... and you were nowhere... I couldn't find you, though I tried... and I tried. I went everywhere we used to go, did everything we used to do... It made no difference; your ghost was always with me, but in every way that mattered, I was alone."

The lovely little girl's tears are running just as fast as mine. She too appears unable to stop the roof from caving in.

"I was there with you, and I tried to reach you, I really did. I swear, Forrester, I did everything I could. I didn't want to leave you."

Wrapping my arms around her more tightly in a loving embrace, I return the sentiment.

"I know, Joy. I know you did, but let us not talk about loss and heartache. Let us celebrate the here and now. We have this time together. It is a gift. Let's not waste it. Let's cherish this second chance at happiness. Let's make this day an adventure, just like we've always done before."

She looks at me with her big, beautiful blue eyes, causing my heart to drop another level deeper inside my chest.

"Alright!" she agrees wholeheartedly. "What would you like to do first?"

As I gaze upon her precious sweetness, I can feel the twinkle returning to my tired eyes.

"Anything you want; although, I'm kind of partial to some candyfloss and, perhaps, a game of chance."

No sooner do I make my intentions known does a loud baritone voice arrive out of the blue handing out invitations.

"Step right up, step right up! Place your wagers down. Spin The Wheel Of Fortune and see where your wishes land."

We look up ahead, no more than twenty steps away, to see a tattered games booth. The canvas wrapped around its wooden frame floats like stray cobwebs on the breeze, and at its centre sits a large wheel, which appears to be rocking back and forth as though stirred by some unseen hand.

"Who said that?" Joy whispers, mirroring my own concern.

"I don't know. I don't see anyone. I don't see anyone here at all. This place looks abandoned in every way except the obvious. There is music playing, I can smell the food and hear all the sounds of the midway, yet I can't see a single thing to lend proof to those other senses. The rides look rusted to the ground, the concession stands are in tatters and the forest has grown up around it all."

"I know what you mean," Joy affirms. "It's almost as though I can hear The Til-ta-whirl spinning and The Ferris Wheel creaking – and I'm sure I can smell popcorn. In fact, the air is heavy with it!"

Though I'm almost too afraid to ask, I make the effort.

"Can you hear the children's laughter too?"

"Yes, I can," she admits. "I was afraid it was only me."

Watching the shadows behind the trees like a hawk, I expect to see Black Bobbin's ghost children emerge out of their dank depths at any moment to descend upon our racing hearts. I can't be certain where the scents and sounds are coming from. They seem far too substantial to merely be imagined; although, I've made that mistake before. Everything appears far too real about this place. I can't even be sure that the one whose hand I'm holding onto and am conversing with isn't anything more than my deepest wish.

"This place sure is creepy. I don't know what to make of it; however, it does look like it would be a fun place to explore. C'mon, let's play a game. I'll spin the wheel. You can make the bet. This place looks to cover quite an area. We can explore it all. It will be just like old times. Remember all the fun we've had over the years at the fair – all the rides we've gone on, all the games we've played, all the candyfloss we've eaten between french fries and ice cream, all the trouble we've caused our parents."

Her crying eyes are soaked with tears again.

"I do remember, Forrester, and it does sound like fun, but this place is spooky. It gives me the creeps. There's something about it that feels so incredibly off – so very unnatural. I don't feel safe here at all. It feels haunted."

She does make a valid point with her effort. The atmosphere in this part of the woods is quite unnerving. It is incredibly unsettled and anything but still.

"I know what you mean," I tell her. "It does feel haunted. I will understand completely if you don't want to do it. We can go around and find something else."

"No, it's alright," she insists calmly. "I would like to spend some time here. It feels good to remember, and I want to remember it all – every moment of our life together... every single thing we said and did and felt during those precious years."

"Well, let's pretend, then. Let's pretend to play a game, and eat candy floss, and then we'll go on some rides. Even if we just sit in them, I'm sure it will feel like we're riding in them again... just the way we used to do."

The lovely little girl agrees in a heartbeat.

"Okay, let's go!" she expresses in cheerful candour.

Hand in hand, we walk over to the nearest games booth, the one with the large spinning wheel of chance. Joy leans against the counter while I duck under the gate to act as games man. I give the big wheel a spin to jump start the fun.

"Well, what do we have here... what do we have here – a new contestant? What do you wager, my dear? How much are you willing to gamble?"

Joy wraps her smile around her words.

"I'm not sure. I'll have to think about it. I don't want to lose anything important."

"But those are the only kind of bets we allow. Would you be willing to wager your heart?" I tease gently.

"Oh, but kind sir, I don't have my heart to risk. It's already been given to another."

I smirk rather sheepishly.

"And would I know that *someone*?"

She winks her words my way.

"Oh, I think you would."

The first spin of the wheel is beginning to slow to a stop, so I feel a need to increase the pressure.

"Fair enough, then. What are you willing to wager?"

Taking a moment to deepen her thought, she eventually decides on an outcome.

"I will wager a wish. If I win, you have to grant it to me."

I don't even have to waste a moment to think about it.

"And if you lose?" I question.

"If I lose, you'll get to kiss me."

This *is* a fun game!

"Alright, I like those odds. I'll take your bet. Pick your poison. What colour do you choose?"

I reach a hand out to stop the wheel before it stops on its own. Next time, I will spin it for real.

A hint of a smile reaches across the lovely girl's lips, and I swear I can see the beginnings of tears forming in the corners of her eyes.

"I choose white because it's the colour of the dress I will wear on our wedding day."

I choke back the lump in my throat and try to pinch off my tear ducts to prevent any sign of my own emotional meltdown. I try to bridge the flood of sadness washing over me with a cheerful reply.

"An excellent choice... Now are you ready to gamble?!"

"I am," she insists.

"Alright, then, let the games begin!"

I pull down with one mighty push, throwing all of my weight into the process, and the wheel of chance embarks upon its lucky rounds. Round and round it goes, spinning crazily like a drunken top. It seems as though it's not content on stopping. It is travelling so fast that I'm afraid it's going to jump clear off its wall and roll away into the forest where it would be sure to get lost for good. The entire structure appears to be vibrating. Things are getting intense! I'm on the verge of asking Joy to back away, for I'm already beginning to fear for her safety, when the sense of relief I've been anticipating pushes itself down from the clouds. The big wobbly wheel begins to slow, easing down with every round, swooping in on its eventual stop.

It passes the white slot... skips across the blue, yellow and green tabs before nearly settling into the red – but no, it's not done yet. As though building up anticipation to its full advantage, it rolls along a little further – across the orange and black notches before dropping purposely into another patiently waiting slice of white. It looks like Joy will have her wish, after all.

I turn to my lovely friend and smile.

"We have a winner! You've wagered wisely; lady luck has smiled your way today."

"Wonderful!" she squeals with glee. "Now you'll have to grant me my wish."

I smile easily, ready and willing to oblige.

"I suppose I will. When exactly do you plan to enlighten me as to the nature of that said wish?" I wonder aloud, unsure what precisely will be expected of me.

"Oh, you need not worry until the time comes. Then I will make it known, and you will have to oblige me," she instructs matter of fact like, though in a very playful manner. It's highly effective; it helps to keep my worry at bay."

We leave the games behind and head for the concession stand. It too looks as though it's seen far better days. The paint is peeling away from its walls and the glass meant for keeping out the elements and holding back the customers is lined heavily with cracks. A few dried up kernels of popcorn strewn about on the shelving and the floor are the only scraps of food in sight. Oddly though, the air is rich in all manner of mouthwatering scents. I can readily smell corn dogs, french fries, cotton candy – and yes, freshly popped buttered popcorn. What's more, I can taste them. It's the most remarkable thing. It's as though I have already eaten and have been left completely satisfied by the meal.

Joy agrees; her taste buds have been equally spoiled. This amusement park might have long since been abandoned, but somehow, it still lives on in a sort of frozen grace. It's not quite dead; it yet holds breath.

We decide to wash down our lunch with some freshly squeezed ice cold lemonade. The sweet tart sensation left in my mouth is no less authentic. It leaves me feeling as though I've just enjoyed the most refreshing beverage of my young life. It's a strange sense to get a hold of. I didn't have to eat a thing; the smells were so vivid that I could practically taste them. I could taste them so well that it satisfied my hunger better than anything I've ever eaten before. All that's missing is a sweet chunk of fudge. We can't resist the temptation and conspire to indulge ourselves to the fullest value of the dollar, though no money need change hands at this carnival. We're riding the midway for free!

"I'm having rum and raisin!" Joy enlightens.

"Mine is Rocky Road!" I return, and the two of us skip our way across the majestic wooded park – all the way over to the nearest amusement ride. Giant trees weave their way between the rusty structures, which appear to have become part of the forest. They reach out their clutching arms, wrapping around the massive trunks.

We arrive at The Tilt-a-whirl and waste no time in running up onto the creaking boardwalk that circles around the bucket seated cars.

"That looks like a good one!" I point out, and Joy confirms the notion.

"I agree; it looks to have plenty of spin in it."

We race over to it as though in a footrace with at least a dozen others and climb into the tattered, worn seat. It takes the two of us pulling down on the safety bar to secure ourselves sufficiently enough to ride, and by throwing our weight from side to side, we are able to scrape off enough rust from the tracks to start the car rocking. Slowly at first, back and forth we roll. Then a little further... then a little more... and before we know it, we're rolling steadily back and forth. And then something truly quite remarkable occurs. We spin completely around in a full cycle – not once, but twice, then again and again! So fast we are spinning that it's making me dizzy. So fast we are spinning that it feels as though we're starting to move. I swear we really are moving. The haunting clusters of sound descending upon our eardrums appears to be growing louder, and the ride we're on seems to be moving along with it. With every spin, we appear to be going a little faster. Before we know it, we've done a complete round – and then another. Everything is just a blur. We raise our arms above our heads and scream as loud as we can. We're like two little kids. We are just the way we always were... all those summers spent together... running through the midways at every country fair.

We turn to look at each other – the smiles on our two faces as wide as the memories we've kept of all those years. We look deep into each other's eyes and see the brilliance – we see the truth of all we share. I truly don't know how I'm going to be able to say goodbye to this little girl... just let her go... back to our world... or leave her behind in this one – if what Black Bobbin claims isn't true. Either way, letting her go a second time – and this time very likely for good – is going to rip my heart out. It will be devastating beyond contemplation.

CHAPTER 16

BROKEN BY WORDS AND BROKEN BY FEELINGS

The ride slows, and the spinning gradually comes to a stop. For a moment, we sit in silence reflecting on the fun we've just shared... gazing at each other fondly and thanking the heavens for granting us one more wish. How many days have I taken for granted? How many careless thoughts got trampled into the dust – when I should have been treasuring each and every moment I had been given with the girl I loved. I can't change it now, though I wish I could. I wish I'd known so I could have done something different, though I'm not sure what I would have done. It was probably better I didn't know. How hard would that have crushed my heart?

Silence is often broken by words, and silence is broken by feelings. This time it is broken by both. Joy sees an opportunity to share the worries that have been plaguing her beautiful mind.

"I would like to tell you something, Forrester," she announces bravely. "I don't want to make you sad or make this harder than it needs to be; however, since coming here, I've had a chance to see things. I've seen many wonderful things and some that are incredibly sad. I've seen the future, Forrester – I've seen our future."

"I've seen it too, Joy. I was there with you. I

saw the life we would have lived."

Joy shakes her head emphatically.

"No, I'm not talking about when we were together down in the tunnel. I mean before... before you got here, when I first arrived, when I was by myself."

"I didn't know you remembered anything from that time. I didn't know... Well, I didn't know what to think."

"It's alright; I didn't say anything because I didn't want to frighten you, but I was here. I remember it clearly. I was all alone and it seemed to last an eternity."

For some reason, I feel it necessary to enlighten her on a few of the facts.

"It was nearly two months, but I know what you mean; it seemed like forever for me too."

She looks at me fondly with tears dripping from dust settled eyes.

"I knew you would miss me... I knew you wouldn't forget."

"I could never forget." I shake my head violently. "All I did was miss you, Joy – from morning till night. Every waking moment was spent searching for you. I went back to all the places we used to go – over and over. Thoughts of you kept me awake at night, and when my tired mind gave in to sleep, you lived inside my dreams. I was desperate, confused, sick without you. I didn't know what to do. I thought I'd lost you for good."

A steady flow of tears is pushing out the corners of her eyes.

"I tried to get back to you, but I couldn't. I was so frightened. I didn't know what to do, so I waited. Time seemed to pass so slowly, but I never gave up. I knew you would come for me... and you did."

"You made it possible. I followed you here."

"But you had to get to that place. If you weren't searching for me, you couldn't have found it."

Joy smiles through her tears.

"It looks like we found each other, then. How perfect is that?"

My simple words can't express the gratitude I truly feel.

"Pretty perfect... I think it was a gift from God."

"It was a gift from something."

With that said, Joy's lips purse together tightly and an odd expression overtakes her eyes. It's come about so sudden, I'm afraid to ask what could have brought about the shift.

"It is no matter; I'm just thankful we've found each other again. I wouldn't trade this time together for the world."

My beautiful girl looks at me seriously and squeezes both my hands.

"Still, there is something I want you to know. When I first got here – when I was alone, I saw our wedding day, I saw the dress I made by hand – every last trace of lace and every bead I sewed in. I felt the pride and love that went into every stitch. I felt what I was feeling when we said our vows. I felt the overwhelming flow of love move through my soul. I knew the happiness inside my heart and saw it in your eyes. I experienced the entire moment as it was truly meant to be. I saw everything that the tunnel didn't show us – and we were happy... I want you to know, Forrester, that we were truly happy. We were blessed. We were meant to have a joyous life together."

The polarizing effect of my mixed feelings is waging war inside my guts. I'm not sure whether I ought to be happy or sad. It's nice to know how wonderful things were meant to be between us, though how can it feel good to know that all of it is lost? How am I supposed to live with that? And what am I left to do now but lie – if that's what I'm really doing. I don't even know that for sure.

"Thank you for sharing that with me, Joy; it gives me hope. Perhaps we still have a chance at such a life. If we can find a way home, anything is possible."

Her gaze trailing towards the ground, her awkward smile mirrors my own sentiments exactly.

"Perhaps... It would be a terrible thing to give up all hope."

Neither of us ought to do that; I believe it's the only thing that has gotten us this far.

"Yes, it would," I agree."We must never stop hoping. We're together again, aren't we? So who is to say what is or isn't possible?"

My little friend smiles in the kind fashion she always has for as long as I can remember.

"Who is to say... Anyhow, I just wanted you to know how much love there was between us. I don't want you to ever forget that. I want you to hold onto everything we had... I want you to know how much I loved you."

With my heart caving in inside my chest, it's all I can do to prevent my words from wanting to falter.

"I know, Joy... I do know... I've always known... and I love you too."

...more than the volume of water the ocean's tide pulls back from the shore... more than we allow time to haunt us... more than birdsong brings Joy to the world... but I think she knows that. There's no sense waving the obvious in her face; things are hard enough as they are.

We throw our arms around each other – I'm not certain which one of us is first or faster. All I know is that it's the continuation of a lifelong embrace. Too far from the back of my mind is the thought that it might be the last. I can't bring myself to completely think it, so I content myself with hanging on for dear life. Neither one of us seems to want to let go. Perhaps we both have the same miserable thoughts racing through our minds. It's alright, my sweet girl; I won't let go of you... I will never let go of you.

With tears beginning to dry on sticky cheeks and bodies grown hot through the act of compression, we finally pull ourselves apart. I lift the safety bar to free us and we make a grand effort to stagger forth once more.

Trying her best to sound cheerful, Joy playfully requests, "Let's have some ice cream! There's an old ice cream cart over there by that clown – the one holding onto the balloons."

CHAPTER 17

ANOTHER HALF DOZEN PINWHEEL SCARES

My heart nearly stops in my chest. From what world did he come from? Standing nearly ten feet tall and wearing polka-dot bloomers, with a large red rubber nose and orange frizzy hair, he looks like a child's worst nightmare. The pasty white makeup splattered all over his face almost hides the truth; however, the pair of hooves anchoring his legs to the ground and the set of horns protruding ever so slightly above his wig leave the nature of his true identity far too clear. Even if those dead giveaways weren't so obvious, the bunch of balloons he is holding in one hand would give away all the rest. On the surface of each one are all of Black Bobbin's children's faces – looking desperate and scared and very much alone... But they're not alone, for I've already joined them; my face is on one.

Joy must see it too, for she looks equally horrified.

"On second thought, why don't we pass," Joy back pedals quickly. "I no longer feel like having ice cream."

"Neither do I," I choke back. "All I want to do is get out of here."

Joy and I nod to one another without

requiring further reply. Grabbing hold of each other's hands, we promptly turn and start running in the other direction. We don't risk looking back, though I can hear Black Bobbin laughing. I fear this little display is his way of reminding me of our unholy bargain. He wants me to know he has no intention of letting me leave this place.

Doing our best to improve our chances of escape, we duck in behind The Merry-Go-Round.

"C'mon, Joy," I encourage. "Let's hide up in there where that creepy clown can't see us. We'll hide there until he leaves."

With burgeoning fear overtaking her eyes, Joy nods in earnest.

"Alright, Forrester, I'll do whatever you ask. I don't want him to find us. He frightens me."

"I won't let him harm you," I try to assure her, though I don't know how I could possibly protect her. How could I – or anyone stop him from doing whatever he wanted? I certainly couldn't hope to here in the heart of his domain. Our best chance is to hide from him – if we can even do that. His eyes and ears are everywhere, and if he can't see or hear us, he can read the thoughts in our heads. There's no escaping his crawling reach. He controls all the children lost in this place, and the animals – their minds are continually bent by his will... Well, perhaps all the animals but one. That fat cat, Jackson Trigg, might prove to be the exception. Where is he when I need him? I could really use his help right about now, though he's probably already given up on me and walked away for good. Perhaps I shouldn't have been so stubborn, but what else could I be? I don't see that I was given much of a choice.

"Just stay close to me and we'll find a way out of here," I promise, though my hope in such an ill-gotten belief is fraying terribly fast. My words of assurance are sounding more and more hollow the deeper into this trap we fall.

Joy nods obediently as I instruct further.

"Quickly now, let's climb up onto the carousel and hide down under the horses' hooves. There are plenty of shadows in there. No one will find us – just as long as we stay quiet and still."

As always, Joy is with me – right by my side in spirit and deed. There is no question; she's as steadfast and loyal a companion as anyone could ever hope to count on. We hop up onto the slick varnished platform, untroubled by wear from the wind, rain and sun, and creep between the prancing saddled steeds. The staunch wooden horses have been carved very true to life and form, with fiery eyes, wide snorting nostrils and shod hooves made to trample and kill. The shadows beneath the carousel's rooftop have grown long and restless. They wrap their fingers around the horses' clenched jaws, pulled back by steel bits, and force their heads down to find us, searching the carousel floor for anything foreign... for anything that doesn't belong.

Their red saddles and painted on bridals roam tightly upon their hot lathered backs. The bays and the roans, chestnuts, buckskins and paints, and shiny blacks and soft, golden palominos all prance and paw their way closer, intent on causing great harm.

"I don't like it in here!" Joy cries in terror. "I don't feel safe on this ride at all!"

I can hear Black Bobbin's devilish footsteps forking into the ground not far off, and the scurrying about and giggling of his small children can be heard even closer. I'm well aware of how frightening this hiding place seems at the moment, but what waits for us out there is sure to be much unkinder still. Just as I'm about to give expression to those thoughts to the lovely frightened girl beside me, something far worse presents itself outside our door. I hear hooves clamour up onto the carousel's platform.

"Click, clack... click, clack, clack..." they tap their way nearer. "Click, clack... clackity click..." they come to a stop.

Suddenly, I'm very aware of the silence. All I can hear is the sound of my pounding heartbeat and the lonely howl of the wind through the trees. I stop breathing, and I know that Joy's done the same. We look at each other and we wait – and we can feel the other shake out of sheer fear and helplessness.

Just when the silence seems intense enough

to kill us by pure pressure upon our hearts, we hear an ominous *click* and The Merry-Go-Round begins to creak. Slowly it starts to turn round in a circle. Round and round, it moves faster, picking up speed. Before we can fully comprehend the danger we're in, it is racing! Round and round, it spins, feeling as though it's out of control.

Holding onto each other, Joy and I grasp hold of a pole piercing through a horse's abdomen. We hang on for dear life while abandoning all further hope for a miracle. We're both content to take it in place of everything else.

"Click, clack, click... clackity clack..." the hooves of the dark loathsome creature scurry between the horses... move closer... weave around gingerly, as though working out the steps of some intricately choreographed waltz. He is pretty surefooted. Any lesser being would have joined us on the floor or been thrown clear long ago.

Fear has the two of us frozen, and what a horrible, helpless feeling it is. I'm so terrified that I'm literally unable to move. I'm not much good to either one of us right now – certainly not to Joy, who is depending upon me for something akin to safekeeping... and certainly not to myself. All I can do is cower in the shadows under the racing wooden horses' hooves and pray he won't find us, though how impossible is that? How can we possibly hope to hide from something like him? As I've stated before, he sees everything, hears everything and lives in our thoughts. He knows where we are before we do. There's no hope of escaping his claws. If he finds us, I know I'll have to face him. I would have no choice; I will defend this sweet little girl to the end... I just hope it doesn't come to that. The part of me that still believes in miracles is holding onto hope that he will somehow miss us down here beneath the wooden horses' hooves, that something will turn his attention towards something else. I don't care what it is. Anything at all would do at this point. The carousel breaking loose from its moorings and rolling across the midway would even be an acceptable choice. The way the ride is shaking, it could happen at any moment. If it does, I only hope that Joy and I are thrown clear.

The two of us hang onto each other for dear life as we cling to the floor of the ride.

"Clackity clack... clackity clack..." Black Bobbin's tap dancing hooves continue to close in on their prey.

Just when fear couldn't have us pinned down any lower, the distraction we've been praying for arrives right on time. I'm not sure who it is at first. We are spinning around much too fast to determine what the white streak is that keeps whizzing past at lightning speed every time we round a corner. However, each time we come around, it gets closer and grows equally in size. Another half dozen pinwheel scares around the bend and I've determined the cause. It's Jackson Trigg! He's proving to be my saviour once again. I think I'm even happier to see him than when I was acting as fish bait in that horrible smelly bog. He did say that he was sworn to protect me. I can thank my lucky stars that he takes the responsibility so seriously. Just when I thought he had given up on me – and I'd seen the last of him, he comes to my rescue one more time.

With my vision dramatically reduced by speed, the large white cat resembles more of a ghost sent to haunt our last moments of life in this world. We're going so fast that his graceful loping appears slow in comparison. I get the sense he is trying to tell me something. He looks as though he wants to get my attention focused his way. I know he wants to communicate with me; I can feel it in my bones. I'm not sure whether it's his voice in my head or not, though if it isn't, I don't see it making any difference; I'm making it out to be as much.

"Get out of there right now, Forrester! Crawl under the horses until you reach the edge of the boardwalk – then jump! Jump as soon as you turn the corner and see me."

I'm quite aware of the possibility that it might be all in my head and I'm only imagining that he's speaking to me. If that's the case of cookies being put on display, then, I'm running quite the risk in contemplating something so blatantly dangerous, yet what danger awaits us by staying here? That devil goat could reach us at any time, and only the worst could come from it, I'm certain of that much. And really, we're running quite a risk either way. Even if it is Jackson's voice telling me what to do, we're risking our lives by attempting it. The trouble is that the alternative seems a little worse.

"Go now!" the voice frantically insists. "Go! Run! Get to the edge, and when you see me, jump!"

Whether it's actually Jackson Trigg's voice or not, it doesn't matter; there is a reason that those words are rattling around inside my head. I'd better listen and act accordingly – in as prompt a manner as my unsteady legs can carry me forward.

I don't have to say a word to Joy. One knowing look into each other's eyes and a squeeze of her hand brings her along for the ride. Where I go, she goes and vice versa. It has always been that way between us, and it always will be – just as long as we're able. It's a quiet understanding between us that's been tested and proven time and time again.

I tug on her arm and give a nod towards the sideboards. As fast as we can crawl on all fours, we weave our way under the wooden horses' galloping hooves and over to the edge of the boardwalk. One spin whips us around in a hurry and all we can do is watch the big white cat fly by as a blur. A second encounter gives us the same, but as we come around for another, Jackson screams it out loud and clear.

"Do it now!"

Before his words have time to fall silent, we're rounding the corner and I'm seeing a streak of snow white fur. Glancing over my shoulder in the same instant, I see Black Bobbin reaching for us, jagged nail-tipped fingers piercing through the air. It's now or never. Torn between what stands for self preservation and what guarantees suicide, I rely on pure instinct. I listen to the voice of the large white cat.

Before Black Bobbin's grappling claws can reach us, we jump... Before The Merry-Go-Round can turn another round of terror, we throw ourselves off the platform into the uncertain abyss – or to be more precise, I jump and take Joy with me. Somersaulting through the air, we narrowly escape the spinning wooden platform we're leaving behind. The whirlwind vacuum being created by the out of control wheel could easily suck us under, crushing us to death in the process. Somehow, though, mercifully, unbeknownst to anything other than grace, we are thrown clear of the gyrating mechanism. The harsh, cutting air grating our flesh like sandpaper as we hurtle towards the ground, we brace for an abrupt landing.

CHAPTER 18

THE WAY HOME

"Poof... ff!"

It's hard to know what to think; it was the last thing I was expecting. If I'd dreamt up such an occasion, I couldn't have imagined a softer landing. It was as though we were caught by a giant feathered pillow or in a net made from silky spider's thread. Jackson somehow managed to get himself under the exact spot he thought we'd fall. By laying his body underneath us, he provided the perfect cushion to ease our landing, and in the process, he very well might have saved our lives. In fact, there is a pretty good chance of it. Hitting the ground at the speed we were travelling, twisting and somersaulting through the air like a pair of runaway tops, we surely would have broken both our necks. The cushioning effect of his soft fur and ample padding made it feel as though we'd been scooped up by a velvet hand. From there, he cradled us until our nervous bodies slowed enough to roll down to the ground. Thankfully, Jackson is as large as he is or else it would have been impossible to cover as much ground as he did to ensure we'd come out of such a perilous situation smiling – or at the very least, alive!

In spite of the giant cat not being able to help me with what I truly want and his insistence that our connection has been severed because of it, he has once again shown up when I've needed him the most, and I am grateful for that. I'm beginning to believe that in this strange world, he's the closest thing I've got to being a guardian angel, though I suppose he ought to have a set of wings for that – and he doesn't look anything like a bird.

Setting my two feet unsteadily back upon the ground, I turn my attention to the object of greatest importance.

"Are you alright?" I ask Joy, while reaching out a hand to help her up.

She appears to be in shock and is slow to respond, prompting the large white feline to wedge his words into the space left by silence. Already back up on all fours, he's barking orders at us like some sort of police dog.

"You have no time for foolishness!" he shouts while nudging me forward with his large head. "Hurry... you must run; you need to get out of here!"

I forgive him for his pushiness, for I know his instructions must be immediately obeyed. We might have escaped the runaway carousel, but we're far from in the clear. Black Bobbin will be coming after us at any moment, and a quick look around me reveals that the ghost children have already begun to close in. Their pale faces and beady black eyes are being drawn to our fear. Give it another minute and we'll be completely surrounded.

I look to the big cat for answers, and this time, he is more than willing to oblige.

"Head for The Ferris Wheel on the other side of that clump of trees. You can see the top of it from here. Pull down on the lever in the control booth and then quickly climb into one of the seats. You will have just enough time before it starts to turn. Be mindful though; you'll have just enough time to get into a seat before it begins to move."

Riding The Ferris Wheel seems all well and good, but I fail to understand how it's going to prevent Black Bobbin from reaching us. All he has to do is wait until we come back down to pounce on us. I can already picture him dragging us kicking and screaming from our seat.

"How is that going to save us?!" I beg. "Wouldn't we be better off running into the forest to find someplace to hide?"

"There is no place you can hide from the likes of him in this world. His reach extends into every dark corner... His gaze can see beneath every stone. Trust me, Forrester; what I am telling you to do is the only answer... I am showing you the way home."

I never thought I'd hear those words spoken, certainly not from that big cat's lips; although, now that I've heard them, I know it's the sound I've been longing to hear. Perhaps it is possible. I'm beginning to believe that Joy and I will get out of here.

"The way home..?" I ask for affirmation.

"Yes, it is the only way for you to get back, but you must hurry. Quickly, you must go now! Do as I say. Climb onto The Ferris Wheel and it will take you home."

"But how?!" I plead for more answers. "What am I supposed to do then?!"

"You'll know when the time comes. It will be apparent. Just get to The Ferris Wheel and it will take you home."

"But why The Ferris Wheel?" I persist.

"It has always been your way out of here, Forrester... It has always been your way back."

With those parting words of encouragement, Jackson Trigg gives me one last push and I rush forward pulling Joy along beside me, too afraid to look behind. The two of us make a run for The Ferris Wheel. I can hear the children's quick little steps coming after us, and Black Bobbin's presence can be felt all around. Somehow, I instinctively know that The Ferris Wheel is the answer. If anything can bring me back... If anything can bring Joy back, that is it. It is a place very dear to both our hearts. It's where we met in the first place. It's where we fell in love. I can still see that little blonde girl sitting beside me holding my hand. I knew I loved her that day and that I would love her for the rest of my life. I just thought I would have more time to do it, that's all. I was under the impression that a lifetime was meant to last forever. I believed that nothing would ever tear us apart.

For a moment, it appears as though we'll never reach it. The trees between us seem content to crowd us out. They wrap their arms around us and nudge us to go round. Even though the top of The Ferris Wheel is now hidden by a ceiling of leaves, I know we must be getting near it; I can hear the seats creaking in the wind. The hollow grating of their skin calls us forward, their haunted spaces waiting to be filled.

"Don't be frightened," I encourage. "It's a lonely place up there, but it's our way out of here. I'm sure of it."

Joy nods and we keep pushing forward, through the branches that creep down to the ground like vines to wrap around our ankles... through the course blades of grass that climb above our heads. We must hurry in one direction regardless of the resistance from without and from within. Black Bobbin's ghost children are closing in behind us. I can hear their footsteps skittering nearer all the time. Out of the corners of my eyes, I watch them, their blank expressions pinching as they laugh. The old goat himself can't be far behind. I can feel it. His dark energy is growing heavy in the air.

With every breath, we move a little further. With every step, we gain a little ground. It feels as though we're moving in slow motion even though I know I'm running just as fast as I can. The dense growth of trees grown up around our destination isn't helping. It seems as though it's been placed before us to stick us here like glue. I can't resist temptation meddling with my thoughts; I can't do anything other than imagine it to be Black Bobbin's doing, for he controls these woods as he does everything else. It is not so outlandish to believe he could bend the trees to his will, make them grow dense and course ahead of our path. I believe that he would do anything in his power to keep us here. I greatly doubt he ever intended to let either one of us go. If he gets to us before we reach The Ferris Wheel, we'll both be stuck in this over grown bramble patch for good, though I'm sure he'll make a point of keeping us apart. I sense he prefers the company of tortured souls above anything else. He will tell me that it's impossible for Joy to be with me. He will insist that she is nothing more than stray thoughts in my head... However, I know otherwise – and that's the only thing that's going to prevent him from having his way.

Our persistence proves worthwhile; the dense layer of trees we've been stuck in thins out as quickly as it poured itself over us in the first place. And just like before, we hardly notice the change until well into something entirely new. Joy and I now find ourselves in a clearing – well, as near to one as we've come in this place. The trees are not far off by any means of the imagination. The small patch of blue sky overhead is the only indication of something different, though I see it as a promise of something much more. I see it as a way out.

Without the trees to hide it, The Ferris Wheel is clearly in front of us. It waits with its creaking resistance, patiently biding its time. The high metal beast rises above the treeline, making it possible to see its top from almost anywhere in the park. It was only when we got too close that it was hidden – as is the way with many things in life, I find. It is much easier to see the truth when viewed from a distance. Getting close only tends to cloud your eyes.

It is an old-fashioned model, one designed using the minimalist approach, the kind with the swinging bucket seats and plenty of open air between you and the ground below. It's the kind of ferris wheel I remember riding on as a kid – the kind that makes your stomach churn the higher up you go. It sure does bring back memories. It takes me back to five years old... scared and exited in equal parts. It's been the defining moment of my life. It was the moment I first laid eyes on Joy. I remember my mother and my grandmother being there, but it was the first time I was sent on a ride all by myself, though I wasn't alone; I had my Joy with me the entire time.

I turn to the same angel beside me, a little older, a little more grown up, but only more lovely.

"Are you ready? We must get on."

"Yes," she answers, "I understand."

But does she? I wonder... How can she when I don't fully understand it myself?

I rush over to the nearest seat gently swaying in the soft breeze, just ever so slightly creaking slowly back and forth... back and forth. It sits empty and inviting, its safety bar open wide to welcome us in. I help Joy into her seat before focusing my attention on the controls. I pause just long enough to draw back the words Jackson Trigg uttered to me. *Pull the lever and get into your seat. There will be just enough time but none to spare.* I don't want to mess this up. I know we're running out of time.

The lever seems to be stuck at first. I have to grab it with both hands and brace myself, but with enough effort, it does begin to move. It feels as though I'm pulling a pea through molasses, but I do manage to shift it.

"Click." It locks into place.

Almost instantly, the gear wheels start turning – and the belts and the chains. Then the whole ferris wheel begins to move. Everything sounds rusty – almost as though it wants to seize up, yet it keeps moving. Joy's seat rises a little higher with every turn of the gear wheel's spokes.

"Hurry, Forrester!" Joy cries out to me.

I do my best to appease her; I'm already halfway there and hurrying with as much speed as my legs will provide. I pull myself up into the seat just before it gets beyond me. Jackson was right; I didn't have much leeway. An instant later and it would have been out of my reach. Talk about living life on the edge... It is a good thing I didn't know how little time I really had or I might have worried myself into missing the boat. I can see that The Ferris Wheel is already moving too fast for me to have caught another chair. I had to get on before it picked up momentum, and I only had seconds to do it. Otherwise, I would've gotten myself killed trying to jump onto this ride.

I swing the safety bar around and lock it in place. With the height we'll be reaching, I want something holding us in. These rocking bucket seats are anything but reassuring. They are far from secure. If we rock too far forward, we could find ourselves dumped clear out of sight. I've never felt entirely safe riding on one of these things.

UP, up, up we travel, faster and much higher than I'd prefer. Like everything else in this place, The Ferris Wheel is gigantic. It has to be to reach above the treeline. It's gaining so much altitude that, I swear, before we're through, we'll be touching the clouds in the sky.

As we race nearer to the tops of the trees, it suddenly dawns on me that we have no way of stopping this thing. We'll go around endlessly until either we run out of fuel or somebody else intervenes and puts a stop to our joyride. I can picture us gaining momentum... going faster and faster until the chairs start spinning out of control... The bolts couldn't hold that kind of tension. The whole thing would come apart for sure. I have no reason to be so worried; I'm sure that Black Bobbin or one of his shadow children will make every effort to bring us down long before it comes to that. Whether they bring us down safely is another matter entirely unto itself. I wouldn't put it past them to speed the ride up in order to shake us loose from our seat. All I know for certain is that they'll want to bring us down. I doubt if they're overly particular about the method.

As we rise above the treetops, I gain a better understanding of the proceedings on the ground below. The ghost children have tracked us here and have already surrounded The Ferris Wheel. A rough count of heads gives me twelve. Black Bobbin's progress has been less concise. Jackson Trigg has put his life on the line to slow him down. The big white cat is locked in what looks to be an intense battle with the horned devil goat. They are repeatedly circling and lunging at one another in a brutal contest of will. Even from this distance away, I gain the impression that horns, claws and teeth are severing flesh.

Jackson does take his duty quite seriously. He's protecting me with his life. You can't get much more serious than that. I'm very aware of how much I owe him. It's not the first time he's saved my life, but it is the first time he's risked his. To oppose Black Bobbin in this world is akin to suicide, and he is doing it for the sole purpose of buying me time. It is a little bit ironic that it's the very thing I came here in search of – and the one thing that Jackson Trigg refused to offer, yet he's giving it to me now when I need it the most.

Reaching as high as we can go, we seem to hang in the air for a moment before going over. In that frozen moment of lapsed time, our momentum seems to roll back a little. The present hesitates. It waits for us to catch up, but we're not ready to continue just yet. The crystalline view is too gorgeous to give up on. All we want to do is make it last.

From our privileged vantage point, at least three hundred feet above the ground, we can see for miles. There are no clearings nearby, as we had hoped to find, only endless treetops. For as far as the eye can see, all there is is forest – an expansive canopy of leaves, glistening green brilliance, ebbing and flowing in one long continuous wave. It has a hypnotic quality to it. The longer you stare into its midst, the more you're tempted to forego all reason and dive right in. Thankfully, the sensation is short lived. I can already feel us beginning our descent over the edge. It's that same stomach dropping feeling I used to always get every time I'd ride The Ferris Wheel. It's a thrill and nausea, both at the same time, but both are equally seductive.

Down... down we plunge, back beneath the treetops. Down, down, the rising ground is in a rush to meet us. It is like a whole other world down below the branches. Dark and hollow... it's as though we're passing below water, its transparent liquid elegy the only constant reminder of the freedom left behind.

It takes mere seconds for us to swoop down

to ground level – less than that to notice all the sets of ugly eyes watching us like hawks deciding what to have for dinner. All fifteen of them must be gathered round *the table* now. Standing between the trees, they look like lanterns about to set the woods ablaze. I never thought that children could be so off-putting as these. Their presence here is so vile and disturbing that all I want to do is run. There is something wholly unnatural about their disposition. They do not come across as innocent at all. They seem to be reaching out to us with their eyes as we pass by them. Their arms remain stationary, as though permanently glued to their sides, with no hope of any other recourse.

The children don't say a word. In fact, the entire forest hangs in silence. There is only Joy's frightened refrain to part the frozen tundra around my ears.

"I don't like those children. They scare me. It feels as though they want to take me somewhere – somewhere I don't want to go."

I know exactly what she means.

"I get the same feeling. There is something unsettling about their eyes. But don't worry; they won't be able to reach us here. As long as we stay on this ferris wheel, we'll be safe. Jackson Trigg said it is the way home."

Looking at me straight on, with just a hint of fear still clinging to the corners of her eyes, she whispers the three words I need to hear.

"I believe you."

As though lifted by those words alone, we ascend upwards through the trees and back into the sunlit tide. The sky is mauve and scarlet, mixed with blues and yellows and hickory bark browns. It is absolutely breathtakingly stunning. It resembles a substance more like water than air... more like cream than cloud... more like heaven than anything else, where as the first time around, all it seemed was unusually blue.

Suddenly becoming distraught, Joy begins to cry. It doesn't take me long to discern what it's all about. Looking down over the treetops, I can see the result of Jackson's intervention. It is not nearly so lovely a sight as what lies above us.

"Oh no!" Joy gasps in horror.

The big noble cat lies in the grass, motionless and bleeding. It is clearly his reward for his good deed done. I feel a great sadness, a profound heaviness in my heart. The thought that he's sacrificed everything for me makes me feel uneasy. I had no right to ask for nearly so much.

My eyes need not travel far to find the one to blame for such injustice. Black Bobbin's dark shadow is moving towards us in a fast and steady line. If something is going to happen, it had better happen soon, or else the devil goat will be upon us and all our running will have gone for not. I don't think he would kill us. I think he'd be content to keep us here... to succumb to deprivation... to watch our eyes become as dead as the other children's.

Down we swoop to do another pass below the trees. Down... down... our stomach's drop with every meter lost or spent behind us. The shadow children seem to be closing in. I'm certain they've dragged their tired bodies nearer, and the woods are growing darker.

Again we rise to see the light. It comes to us like morning – before we plunge a third time round, just to remind us of what we're fleeing. Black Bobbin's spectre has reached us now. All the leaves have curled up... gnarled and twisted on their limbs. I shudder at his sight, for I know he's come to collect what's owed him, though I'm not sure I'm prepared to pay the price. I can feel Joy shaking in her seat beside me. I know it's pure fear she's feeling; I'm feeling it just as much.

The black devil is reaching for the control lever. He could increase our speed ten times over. He could kill us if he wanted to. Perhaps part of me hopes he does. Maybe that's what Jackson Trigg meant by *going home*. It might be our only way out of here.

We once more climb the emerald staircase, the green leaves fluttering by us in alarming haste. Above the treetops we curve upwards, breaking through the barrier that separates that which is possessed by land from sky. And just as we reach our highest destination, at the point just before our seat takes its long plunge down... the place where I

can see more clearly than I have ever seen before...
Actually, there is one other time my vision has
reached so far. When I stood among the rafters,
looking down between the boards, way up high in
the haymow of that old barn towering above the
meadow... That's the only other time I've seen so
far.

The view is endless. The green shellac of
leaves appears to go on forever, like a sea of grass
beneath the sky, which is filled with stars now,
though it's clearly day, not night. Whereas the
world beneath us stays stagnant, everything changes
constantly up here.

CHAPTER 19

TIMOTHY FIELDS AND THE WAVING BARLEY FLOOD

"Ooooff!"

The wind is driven from my lungs in an instant. We've both been thrown up against the safety bar. The ride has stopped with a suddenness that could not be anticipated or braced for. It very nearly throws the two of us out of our seats. Joy almost does go over. I have to grab her by her arm to hold her in.

"Aah!" she screams. "I'm falling!"

"I've got you!" I reassure. "Hold on! We'll be alright. We've just stopped suddenly, that's all."

That's all?! *We've been stopped* is closer to the truth, and what's about to happen next is anyone's guess, and there's a good chance that it's not going to be good. But what's the point of stacking more worry on an already pronounced pile? Another thought like that would push us out of our seats for sure.

We fall back into our seats and cling there, bracing ourselves against the frame, each other – whatever we can find that seems secure... And here we sit rocking back and forth – far more quickly than is good for our nerves. The abrupt stop has caused such forward momentum that our seat is twisting from side to side beneath us. Thankfully, eventually it will have to stop. It's a gradual letup, but it appears as though our expectations will not go unfulfilled. Eventually, we are going to stop. I can feel our out of control motion easing up already. If only we could do the same with our fear. Swinging slowly back and forth, we hang here, high above the forest... far too afraid to chance looking down. Rocking slowly back and forth, all we can hear is the worrisome creaking of our seat, and the thought of the rusty bolts that hold it together won't give my mind a moment's peace. I'm faced with the horrible truth of how things are. The seat we're in could let go at any time. Perhaps Black Bobbin does mean to kill us both... if Joy can die more than once.

The rocking slows down to a quiet pulse. If we weren't so high above the ground, my heart rate might ease a beat or two. As it stands, I'm still on edge. There is nothing safe about the situation we're in, and Joy and I both know it. She is squeezed up close and holding onto me for dear life. Her entire body is shaking. I know I'm going to have to make a choice. Our day in the sun is over. The time given has run its course... and now that black devil awaits his payment. It's the moment I've been dreading all along. I must say, though, it was worth it. It was worth any price just to have one more day.

Looking through the visceral rain that's really just heat condensation rising off the forest, I can see my mother, and father, and little sister. I can see our farm on Cabot's Hill, and Barrett's Meadow and the run down Kennedy Homestead, with the old rope swing on the tree out front. I wish we were on that swing right now instead of this one; I'd feel ten times more secure. It's closer to the ground, for sure.

"Do you see it, Joy?! Can you see our home?!" I exclaim in excitement.

I want affirmation that I'm not just imagining my desired outcome.

"Yes, I do. It looks wonderful."

"Jackson Trigg was right; this is the way home. But it's so far ahead. How are we going to reach it?"

It's as though the sky has been torn, and behind that tear is our world... only separated by the thinnest of veils. It appears so close yet so far away. It's at least a good twenty meters ahead of us. Even if The Ferris Wheel starts to turn again, we'll never get near enough to reach it.

Joy looks at me and smiles.

"Don't worry; there is a way and it will be shown. Just hold onto your faith. Jackson Trigg was right; this was always the way home."

I'm glad she possesses such certainty, though I'm finding it hard not to doubt. Nothing has worked out as I hoped it would. None of it was supposed to turn out this way. She doesn't know about the bargain I've made with that horned devil down there – the one manipulating all the strings like some deranged puppet master hellbent on nurturing a deprived existence where all his nightmares grow fruit and metastasize inwards. She doesn't know that only one of us can go home.

"I know there's a way, and I know that all it takes is faith. I do know that. I'm just not sure that I'm ready."

The terrible truth, which is riding side saddle with both pistols drawn and pointing at my temples, is that I can already hear Black Bobbin's whispers in my head telling me that a choice must be made, insisting upon my senses that my refusal to take action will result in both our deaths.

Taking a chance and peering over my shoulder at the danger that awaits us below, I see proof that I'm not mistaken the sounds. I see Black Bobbin's glowing red eyes staring up at us, and I see his hand on the control lever, and I hear his voice in my head continue its dire warning.

"You must choose now. Only one of you can go home. You need to make a decision. If you don't, both of you will perish. That is a certainty."

I know I've already made my decision; I've known it all along. For Joy to have another shot at life, I would give up my own... I would give anything.

As I stare at the devil who is forcing me to make such a choice, I find it odd how, looking down upon him from this height, Black Bobbin appears to be no more than a tiny black goat. Gradually, from out of the corners, another voice, cloaked in a kinder and gentler tone, wedges its way into my thoughts. It can be no other than my friend the white cat's.

"Don't look down. Only look towards home. It is the only way."

Oddly, I know enough to listen. Looking back was only making me queasy. I also know I'm holding Joy's hand for the last time. I've got to brace myself before letting go. Before going through with this, I must accept her not being here.

"Of course you're ready," she gently insists. "You have done everything that you came here to do. You needed more time and it was given. In this world, in only a few moments together, we've known a lifetime. No matter what happens now, it will be alright. Every moment we shared was worth it. Always know that."

I appreciate the sincere comfort in her words, but logic and reason don't mean a thing to a broken heart.

"But I don't want to lose you," I plead as my heart is breaking further. "I want us to go home together."

The lovely girl looks at me with pure love in her eyes.

"This is home, Forrester. It has always been home. Look around us. Look at the beautiful sky. It is every colour the sky has ever been. Look at where we are. It's the place we first met, where we saw each other for the first time and knew that we could never part. It is the place where all our memories live, every defining moment we've shared, every moment of life in between that has meant just as much. Think about it, Forrester. Where else could you be but home? Where else could any of this exist?"

I'm having a hard time comprehending what she's trying to tell me.

"But that is our home." I point towards the hole in the sky and the thinning ozone. "That's where we come from. It's where we belong. It's where the two of us were meant to live out our lives together."

Joy's lips curl up at the corners and point towards the twinkle in her eyes.

"These two worlds are part of the same. They are not so separate. This one just lies a little closer to your heart. Look, Forrester," she implores upon my troubled mind. "Tell me what you see."

Unless my eyes are deceiving me, she speaks the truth. The once seemingly impenetrable veil separating the two worlds is evaporating right in front of us. The hole in the midst of the sky is growing broader, and I can see more and more of the place I know as home... the timothy fields and the waving barley flood... Lorna Paul's herd of jersey cows grazing in Barrett's Meadow... my mother and father kneeling beside my bed praying... Where else could it be but home?

"But what about this strange place? What about Black Bobbin and Jackson Trigg and the rabbits – and all the other odd creatures here? Where have they come from? I've never seen them before."

The lovely little girl sends a knowing wink my way.

"Haven't you, Forrester? They've been here all along, just like me. You've known them forever."

I'm at a loss.

"What do you mean? I don't understand; I've never seen them before in my life."

"They are all old friends who have lived with you for ages, and they've all served a vitally important purpose here. We've all done our part to bring you back. It is what all of this has been for, everything you've seen and done. It was all part of getting you here."

"I still don't understand."

"You will."

Joy looks into my eyes deeper than ever before and holds onto my hands with more purpose.

"Thank you for sharing this life. It truly meant the world to me. What we've shared will never end. Whenever your heart is low, just remember. If you look for it, you will see. We'll always be coming around on this ferris wheel – two little kids falling in love. You'll always find the two of us on Cabot's Hill or down among the reeds in Barrett's Meadow. You'll find us in the life we would have lived if time had been a little kinder. You'll hear us on the whispering wind. When you think of us, your thoughts will always lead you home."

I'm fighting back my tears, though poorly winning.

"To me, you will always be my home. It's been a real privilege knowing you, Kid. I only wish we'd had more time."

She need not bother with a smile; her eyes are smiling warmth straight through me to the bone.

"We've got forever."

I want to believe her; however, I'm still having a hard time accepting the truth.

"But how do I know that what I'm seeing now is even real? How do I know that you are real? The cat said that I was only imaging you. He said that you weren't even here. And that horned devil creature, Black Bobbin, said the same thing, that you couldn't exist because you were dead. He made you out to be nothing more than a ghost in my head."

"Trust me when I tell you that it was necessary – everything you saw, everything you felt, all the things you experienced here, you needed to see and feel... You needed to have those thoughts. It was all part of getting you to this place."

She still hasn't answered my question.

"But are you real?"

I wait for her lips to open, and it seems like forever for her voice to speak. On the tail-end of anticipation, the beautiful girl whispers her words softly.

"I'm as real as real can be... to your heart, Forrester, so does the rest truly matter?"

"No, I guess not," is my answer.

I didn't need to think it through. It really doesn't matter; I know she will always be with me.

"Then, I will always be there."

The little girl I've loved for ages, the one who I swore I'd never part from, is asking me to do just that. She's telling me that this has been a final reckoning of sorts – a coming to terms with all I've lost... one last gift to see me through. These last few days, or however long I've been here, have seemed real – as real as all the time we spent together back home. As far as I'm concerned, she was here – and still is... She's beside me, holding me right now. I asked for more time with her and it was given, however it might have occurred. It doesn't matter who was responsible for that or the means it was delivered. I'll accept it for what it is, a gift from God.

The little angel sent down from heaven raises herself from her seat. The fragile metal bench we're in once more begins to rock. All the fear I'd forgotten for the moment comes back to haunt me. I'm fearful to look up but even more afraid to look back down. Whether any of this is real or not, it feels as though we're hundreds of feet above the ground. My heart is racing, my stomach's churning, my head is spinning round, and Joy is reaching out a hand to guide me. She's asking me to take one more startling leap of faith.

She sees my hesitation.

"If you believe, Forrester, we can both make it home."

In spite of my mind, body and soul trembling, despite everything in the world holding me down, I summon enough courage to stand. With the unsteady metal surface beneath my feet swaying, with the cool wind blowing through my hair, I put all my belief into this one fragile moment and forget the rest. I don't worry about Black Bobbin or his children. I don't bother to look down; I know there is nothing there now. I hold my breath and squeeze Joy's hand while kissing her gently on her cheek.

"I love you, Joy," I whisper softly, and she says she loves me back... and we jump... We throw ourselves over for the sake of going home.

I don't remember much about the fall, just coming to on the hard barn floor beneath the hay shoot. My mother was there, and my father too, with my little sister, Kaitlin. She was standing there holding Joy's white kitten.

It was quite a tumble, all the way down from four mows up. I fell from the highest barn in the county, with only a thin layer of hay standing between me and the hard concrete floor – just enough to break my fall. Apparently, it was the only thing that saved me. It took several hours for my parents to find me. Quite amazingly, no bones were broken; although, my head and body were badly bruised. It seems I was unconscious the entire time. All who have heard about my near tragedy marvel at how I cheated death. They think it was a miracle. Some are certain I died and came back to life, while other more grounded folk sum it up as lucky. But mostly, my family are just grateful to have me alive and with them. My father never says a thing about moving on and forgetting *my little friend* again. After coming so close himself, he's gained a better understanding of what it means to lose someone... And I've gained the precious knowledge that in order to live life fully, one must keep the things they love most alive inside their heart, for there is nothing in life more real.

After a time, I make my way back to the barn I fell from, but it doesn't look the same. It isn't as I remember it, though nothing ever is, I suppose. But I'm alright with that, for I know the truth... and I'm finally able to let go.

Green fields around you,

stars in your eyes...

Your laugh... your smile,

your sparkling blue eyes...

I see all of your sides,

I see all of your sides.

Lakeside in summer,

black birds in the sky,

and all along... all summer long,

we knew it would be gone.

Little girls playing in the sand,

holding their sister's hand.

Run away... day after day,

under the lilac sky,

and all along... all summer long,

we knew it would be gone.

JOYFIELD

Grandpa's hats,

baked potato snaps,

cross-legged pretzel girls on white sand shores...

Dance away to your secret hideaway.

Come back when you can,

and all along... all summer long,

we knew it would be gone.

Green fields around you,

stars in your eyes...

Your laugh... your smile,

your sparkling blue eyes.

ABOUT THE AUTHOR

RUDSDALE FERRIER grew up on a fourth generation family farm in rural Eastern Ontario, attended Queen's University in Kingston and continues to call the Canadian countryside home. When he's not tending to his herd of Belted Galloway cattle or writing his latest novel, he's an avid runner and tennis player.